TROUBLED WATER

DEVOTION SERIES
BOOK 3

TRACEY JERALD

TROUBLED WATER

COPYRIGHT

DEDICATION

To my beloved, Nathan.
I'll face any trouble head on so long as you're standing beside me.
I love you.

ALSO BY TRACEY JERALD

DEVOTION SERIES

Ripple Effect—Cal and Libby

Flood Tide—Sam and Iris

Troubled Water—Parker and Bethany

AMARYLLIS SERIES

Free to Dream—Caleb and Cassidy

Free to Run—Keene and Alison

Free to Rejoice—Jason and Phil

Free to Breathe—Colby and Corinna

Free to Believe—Jacob and Emily

Free to Live—Joseph and Holly

Free to Dance—Marco and Lynne

Free to Wish—Finn and Jenna

Free to Protect—Brett and Jillian

Free to Reunite—Benedict and Kelsey

AMARYLLIS HERITAGE

Free to Fall—Liam and Laura

Free to Judge—Declan and Kalie

MIDAS SERIES

Perfect Proposal—David and Carys

Perfect Assumption—Ward and Angela

Perfect Composition—Beckett and Paige

Perfect Order—Kane and Leanne

Perfect Satisfaction—Arek and Ursula

Perfectly Free—Brendan and Danielle

Perfect Pitch—Mitch and Austyn

Perfect Pursuit—Ethan and Fallon

GLACIER ADVENTURE SERIES

Return by Air—Jennings and Kara

Return by Land—Kody and Meadow

Return by Sea—Nicholas and Maris

Return by Fire—Jed and Dean

STANDALONES

Close Match—Montague and Evangeline

The Ultimate Challenge—Jonas and Trina & Julian & Elle

Go to https://www.traceyjerald.com/ for all buy links!

PERSONAL COMFORT WARNING

This story is a standalone in the Devotion Series.

The Devotion Series may cause the reader to experience emotional triggers. In this book, the following may occur on page or be alluded to:

- Secret identities
- Emotional scars
- One person not feeling good enough for the other
- Alcohol use
- Family secrets
- Marriage on the rocks
- Reference to kidnapping
- Violence
- Potential loss of child
- Suspense
- Wounded heroine

As always, to enhance your experience, please check the author's website for any personal comfort triggers for the entire series.

PLAYLIST

Luke Bryan: "Kick the Dust Up"
Edwin McCain: "Solitude"
Hootie & The Blowfish: "For What It's Worth"
Metallica: "Enter Sandman"
Kelly Clarkson: "Miss Independent"
Imagine Dragons: "Thunder"
Shania Twain: "That Don't Impress Me Much"
Maren Morris: "80s Mercedes"
Chris Stapleton: "Parachute"
Men At Work: "It's A Mistake"
OneRepublic: "Apologize"

EPIGRAPH

Never let a problem to be solved become more important than a person to be loved.

LEO F. BUSCAGLIA

1

Present QUESTIONS

PARKER

There's three of them in the room with me this time. In light of last night's events, I suppose I shouldn't be surprised.

In the place in my mind where no one believes I have a sense of humor, I secretly wish they'd shown up for this grievous inconvenience wearing red, blue, and green so I could have mocked them throughout the day by addressing them as Alvin, Simon, and Theodore, but alas, they're all dressed in black suits with white shirts. Instead, I drawl, "If it isn't my own little MIBs."

They roll their eyes even as they do checks on the equipment that will be used to perform a rectal probe on me very soon. My arms akimbo, I study them, measuring their skills and ensuring they're not missing a step because of who I am.

"Sir, please take a seat."

With that, I'm gestured forward. My feet don't make a single sound as I move across the concrete floor, past the two-way window where I know people are standing witness to what's about to happen in this room.

They have to, regardless of how they may or may not feel about me as a person, a colleague, or a friend. It's not just their job, it's their patriotic duty to protect the interests of the United States of America.

I expect no less from each of them than what I endure myself, which is why I didn't complain about my discomfort when I was forced to strip out of my custom Saville Row suit of armor in front of watchful eyes before I was forced into the thin, black track suit that is barely big enough to stretch around my biceps. I don't offer any complaints while they meticulously hook me up to machines designed to measure various medical readouts. I stoically endure the pinch between my butt cheeks as the pressure sensor nestles against my rectum as straps are tied around my ankles.

Calves and thighs.

Waist and arms.

And most importantly, around my head and heart.

Lord knows this isn't my first time in the hot seat. I recall the first time I made my way to the center of this very room where—just like now—only one chair, a mess of wires, and a spotlight directly overhead pointed down into my face.

Back then, an agent was debriefing a mere SEAL commander. I was a man who had helped rescue the scarce number of survivors from an at sea hostage situation.

Now, I'm someone completely different.

Even as the first agent begins the rote instructions, I muse, who knew then that the events of the *Sea Force* would alter the course of my entire life down to the fact I'd willingly sacrifice American lives to protect one?

"Sir, my name is Agent Fox. I'll be responsible for asking your questions today. Agents Pamola and Deere are also in the room. They will be monitoring your responses and medical output."

I nod at each of the agents in question. Agent Fox peers down at me. "Are you ready to begin?"

"Yes."

"We'd like to ask you a few baseline questions to calibrate the machine."

"Fine."

"The first two answer truthfully. For the third, we would like you to lie."

"Go ahead."

"What is your name?"

"Parker Thornton."

"Are you married?"

"Yes."

"Have you ever killed an individual intentionally?" The agent looks at me expectantly.

I pause a half a heartbeat. I've killed. I've killed so many times I can't recall the exact number. I've killed because of duty, assignment, mission. But the way they phrased the question? "No."

Agent Pamola's head whips up so fast, I'm certain she's libel to claim workman's comp for whiplash as my lie registers. Besides, it's true. I did kill someone intentionally.

It was last night.

"For what it's worth?"

"Yes?"

"I think my response may address the question you may have been planning to ask. The 'What significant life events have influenced your personal development?' one," I offer. Anything to get this circus act over and done with.

"Not. Even. Close. Sir." Fox glares down at me. Her eyes dip to the base of my throat as if she's measuring it to wrap her fingers around and squeeze. She spins away on her heel to regain her composure. I glance at the clock on the wall behind her. We're a mere six minutes in, and I've already pissed people off. *Impressive.*

This must be a new record of some kind.

Sadistically, I hope the person behind the glass is keeping score because as much as I annoy the shit out of him on a regular basis, it ain't nothing on what's going to happen in this room today. I drawl, "Do you want to ask me my favorite color? Did I have any stuffed animals growing up? What my favorite childhood beach was?"

Fox taps her nails against the desk, "Actually, now that you mention it..."

I get as comfortable as I can, with a smirk on my face and ready to answer whatever question they throw at me.

"What is your wife's name?"

"Bethany."

"Where did Bethany grow up?"

"Kensington, Texas."

"What about you?"

"I was born and raised in Virginia Beach, Virginia."

"Good parents?"

"Great ones. I miss them every day. The car crash that took their life was a tragedy."

"Good influence?"

"Yes."

"Good schools?"

"Excellent. Top of my class in high school, I attended the Naval Academy before graduating and being assigned to BUD/S on Coronado Island."

"Popular."

"Depends on who you ask," I answer honestly.

Fox snickers. "Fair response. So, overall, would you say you had a good childhood?"

"Yes."

"What about your wife?"

Fuck.

2

In the PAST

Bethany

"I don't want to go on living like this!" my father shouts, tears dripping down his face.

He's not the only one shedding them. I've reached for the tissue box so many times I've lost count as my father relives the horrifying moments of watching my mother die before being brutally tortured himself during the anniversary cruise he and my mother took to celebrate their twenty-fifth wedding anniversary.

They left together ridiculously in love, but only a shell of my father returned, carried off by the Navy SEALs who rescued him and few others who weren't murdered in an attempt to rob the *Sea Force*, a luxury cruise liner.

Dad regains his composure as much as he can before he whispers, "But if I'd given in to those terrors, what would have happened to Libby?"

Dr. Bern Powell, a well recognized television interviewer, gives him a chance to regroup by lobbing him a softball of a question. "You're referring to Elizabeth Akin Sullivan?"

Dad nods. "From the start of our voyage, she was all alone. It wasn't until later, after we all returned to land, that I understood why." His face twists. "She lost so much to save so few of us."

Dr. Powell checks his notes. "She credits you, Linc."

He scoffs, "For what?"

"For being alive today."

My father visibly jolts. Hearing Dr. Powell say that makes me want to meet Elizabeth Sullivan even more than I did after hearing my father laud her strength. Before the trip, my father's love and devotion was to my mother, his family, and the business he built up from the back of a pickup truck to a multi-million-dollar enterprise. Since the time he was tortured on the *Sea Force*, and losing Mama to the attack that took place, the only thing that sparks that note of admiration is talk of Elizabeth Akin. She's replaced all of us.

I don't know whether to thank her or hate her.

Dr. Powell tips the scales—at least for today—when he reads aloud, "Elizabeth Sullivan unequivocally states, 'Were it not for Linc McCallister, there is no way I would have endured those hours. His bravery, in spite of his personal devastation, was my touchstone. In rare moments of lucidity, I was heartbroken for Linc about losing his wife, Camille. Twenty-five years of devotion lost because of someone else's greed. He helped me wage a war I wasn't certain I had the strength left to fight, yet what did I offer him?'"

"A path home to my family," my father returns immediately before he physically deflates and mutters, "What was left of it after Camille was murdered."

Did you really come home, Dad? I wonder silently as I take in the closed off expressions of my siblings.

We're all gathered around as Dr. Powell interviews our father for the five-year anniversary special for the events he endured aboard the *Sea Force*. Dredging up memories we work every day to help our father put behind him.

Fortunately, Dr. Powell asks him to expand upon his response, leaving us stunned by our father's words. "I'm not certain I wouldn't have committed suicide aboard that ship if it wasn't for Libby." My father's lips curve. "Knowing her briefly, Cam remarked she felt like she'd known Libby forever. Forever was just cut too short."

I surge to my feet, unable to listen to another word of how my father was willing to abandon us because he just didn't love us enough. It's Dr. Powell who questions my palpitating anger and queries, "Bethany? Do you have something to add?"

With a quick jerk of my head, I storm to the doors leading to the wraparound porch. I need to be far away from the tumultuous emotions my father has stirred up. Once I suck in some fresh air and overlook a field of sunflowers—the natural border between our land and the town founder's property, I feel the ache in between my breasts ease. *God, Mama, I miss you too. I get what happened to you and Dad was beyond devastating. You were murdered. Dad was tortured. People died. But can't the world see it's the survivors who are still suffering? Why can't anyone ask us how we're doing?*

Why can't Dad?

There's obviously no answer. Still, being away from the agony of remembrance gives me a moment's peace. My head falls forward, my long blond hair covering my face. Since I have a modicum of privacy, I let the rare tears I'm allowed to shed drip down my cheeks and land on the plants just off the railing. I think of all the milestones I've given up—homecomings, proms, dates, hell, even walking at my fucking graduation ceremony just so I could take care of my siblings because my father was too lost in his memories to see his family falling apart in the present.

I never knew love could be selfish until then. That wasn't what Camille and Lincoln McCallister taught their children, but Linc

McCallister sure as hell taught us life is. Bitterness almost swallows me when I think about the number of college acceptances I received to some of the best architecture schools in the country—Cornell, Rice, MIT. Turning them all down last year was agony, knowing I was going to be needed right here to raise what's left of his family and keep his company running as he continued to steep himself in mourning.

Long moments later, I hear footsteps on the deck. Judging by the cadence of the footfalls, I know it's my father. Physical therapy made it so he can walk, but he'll never be in the same physical condition he was before he and my mother went on that ill-fated vacation. I don't bother to acknowledge him as he approaches. When he reaches my side, I catch through my curtain of hair he makes to lay a hand on my shoulder. "Bethany, I know it's difficult to hear about how your mother died. I miss her too. Every damn day."

I step back before his fingers touch me and face him head on. He flinches slightly, something he does every time he's forced to look me directly in the face. *It's not my fault I look so much like my mother,* I think resentfully. I'm certain I was told that by every single person who lived here in Kensington, Texas, the day of my mother's funeral after they released her body to be buried.

Five years is an awful lot of time to resent your own face in the mirror.

"I'd like to have Dr. Bern film his wrap up."

He sputters, "But we're not even close to being done."

My voice is flat when I say, "Ellie and Abe have a school presentation due today before their PSAT testing. Jordan has two AP tests."

"Why didn't you say something? I would have..."

I cut him off before he can insinuate he would have listened to me. "What? Listened?"

"Well...yes."

I nod a couple of times before I ask, "Dad, when's my graduation?"

The question takes him aback. "Your graduation?"

"Yes. From high school. Do you know when it is?"

"A few weeks. Make certain I don't forget it." His trembling hand reaches for mine. Again, I step away. He frowns. "What's your problem, Bethany? I won't miss it."

I catch sight of Dr. Powell over his shoulder. Hoping, praying the renowned psychologist can get through to him even if I can't, I allow my agony to show. "You already did, Dad. It was a year ago. Now, I have to get the kids to school before I go to work."

He's a statue, but Dr. Powell asks me, "Work, Bethany?"

"Yes. I've been working at McCallister Construction since I graduated. I take night classes at a local branch of UT."

My father, shaken, snaps, "What the hell happened to your grades, young lady?"

I fling a cold glare in his direction. "Nothing. I got accepted at every school I applied to."

"Then why the hell aren't you there?"

"Because I couldn't trust you to be present for my brothers and sister. Just the fact you didn't even recall that I graduated last year is proof enough I was right." With that, I sidestep him and make my way back inside to wrap up our part in this little farce.

3

Present QUESTIONS

PARKER

"So, you actually knew your wife from a young age."

I correct Agent Fox, "No."

"What would you call it then?"

"I knew of her existence due to a mission brief."

"Can you expand on that?"

I fling a filthy look in Fox's direction because it's not as if what we're discussing wasn't mentioned all over the news in interview after interview for years. "When I was a SEAL commander, I was on the team that helped take out a group of terrorists on board the passenger cruise liner, the *Sea Force*."

"Ah, yes. The *Sea Force*. Isn't that why you resigned your commission?"

"Yes."

"Why's that?"

I think back to the woman I met on board the *Sea Force* and how her fears changed the course of my life. With a deep breath, I admit, "I met Libby Sullivan."

4

THIRTEEN YEARS AGO— AGE 30

In the PAST

PARKER

"What do you mean, you resigned your commission, Thorn? Being a SEAL meant everything to you," Libby asks me with a concerned frown. She rocks back and forth, rubbing her hand over her protruding stomach. A blind idiot can see the bliss that's imprinted on her features.

And I'm certainly not that.

Even though her marriage was rocky when I first met her on the deck of the *USS Lassen* after being rescued from her solo vacation on the *Sea Force*, Elizabeth "Libby" Akin Sullivan obviously took my words to heart. She took the card I handed her with our personal SEAL team psychiatrist's information, thanked me, and proceeded to navigate past the boulders in her life.

Now, she's even more beautiful than I remember, with love

lighting up her features—a deep and endless love for her husband, Calhoun. Not for the first time since I met her, I wonder what it would be like to have Libby's strength and devotion to protect. "Not everything."

"Close," she fires back.

"I got a different job offer. It's...intriguing."

Libby straightens in her rocker. "Really?"

"Yes."

Dr. Rhumed, who fixes our broken minds after every mission, which is why I thought he could help Libby, has asked me if it was Libby I was so enamored of or if it was someone like her—someone who possessed many of the same characteristics my own mother has. The iron core wrapped in a beautiful package. A woman of uncompromising morality. A woman who didn't search for the easy way out but would fight by her partner's side.

To date, Libby is the closest woman I've ever had the fortune of coming across to meet those standards and it worries me that her heart belongs to a man who lied to her from the moment they met. Still, it's a pleasant surprise to know it's not Libby, herself, I want. My only feelings for her are a deep friendship, even though at first I wondered if she wasn't with Cal if it could have been something else.

Who knows? It never was the case. She has always been his.

It's one of the many reasons I may respect the job Cal does—did —as a covert government contractor who covered my ass on more than one occasion. I respect him. Hell, I even consider him a friend. But I'll never hold the same level of respect for him as I do for his wife, considering what drew me to her.

A smirk crosses my face as I find myself staring across the yard where Cal took their monster-sized dog, Darcy, for a walk in the DC suburbs. "Surprisingly, I'll be in less danger in my new role."

Libby hums. "Can you talk about what you will be doing?"

Just then the screen door opens and slams shut. There's the jingle of dog tags before Darcy takes off in a mad dash in my direction. I huff out a choked laugh when he lands on me—all ninety pounds in one fell swoop. "Who trained this mutt again?"

Cal saunters over to his wife and brushes his lips against her forehead, placing his hand against her stomach. The product of their love lets out a hell of a kick as I observe the force that moves Cal's hand. Taking careful note of the open adoration on Cal's face and then Libby's gorgeous face flushes when he murmurs something in her ear I can't quite make out, I couldn't be happier the worst is behind them and they have this upcoming blessing to look forward to. Cal's eyes gleam with amusement when he meets my gaze with wry amusement. "Libby's brother, Josh." He crosses behind her before joining her to face me, sitting in the double rocker.

Libby chimes in with more detail. "He only got around to potty training Darcy."

Cal wraps his arm around her shoulder and she snuggles against him. "To be fair, Libs, that is all you negotiated with him."

I quirk a brow. "You negotiated..."

Libby shrugs. "Josh wanted me to talk to Cal when things between us were...strained. So, he bartered potty training Darcy while I was away on vacation."

A haunted expression flashes across Cal's face so fast, I'd miss it if I wasn't watching him carefully. I align the age of their dog with that nuance and add one and one together. "It was when you were on the *Sea Force*."

Libby nods. Thoughtfully she regards me. "You know, I'm not certain if I ever thanked you, Thorn."

"For what?" I lift the glass of sweet tea Libby had poured earlier to my lips.

"For saving our marriage."

I really wish I'd swallowed before asking her that question. The tea comes spraying out in all directions, hitting the top of the table and Cal's bare leg. "Excuse me?" Me? I saved their marriage?

Cal glares at me before he lets go of his wife, leans forward, and snatches up a cocktail napkin to wipe up the mess. "Don't sound so surprised, Thorn."

"I'm flabbergasted. If I'd known I was a marriage counselor, I'd have added it to my CV a long time ago."

Cal throws up his middle finger in my direction even as Libby chides him for being rude. She amends her statement, "I mean by introducing me to Dr. Rhumed."

"Ahh, that. You know I wanted—want—nothing but the best for you, Libby." My voice gentles at the end. Cal glowers. I smile beatifically in his direction over his reaction. I seriously enjoy the fuck out of getting a rise out of him.

Notwithstanding our friendship now, I still harbor some lingering resentment against him. After all, he practiced at being a professional liar—not that it didn't help me on more than one occasion. Still, those lies almost blew up his own marriage. My expression must reflect my inner thoughts because Cal's face takes on a rueful cast.

Libby informs me, "We spoke with Dr. Bern a few weeks ago for the five-year anniversary special."

"I'm impressed you did any interviews." I let the Navy Media Relations office handle my statement, much as I did for all the interviews conducted after the events of that week.

Cal sits back and wraps Libby back up in his arms. "It was healing."

I shoot back. "It took away your anonymity, Sullivan."

He looks me straight in the eye. "I don't need it anymore. Not with the job, not to protect Libby."

No, I guess he doesn't. Shortly after the events that almost ripped Libby and Cal's lives apart, Cal's company was approached for a takeover by Hudson Investigations. Cal, in addition to owning part of the lucrative firm, now heads their Missing Children division. I've heard from my contacts that it not only gives him a taste of the old life but also puts his best talents to use.

I'll have to remember that for the future in my new role.

Libby talks about how she spoke about our shared psychiatrist in a general sense and also gives me a bit more insight about how much she's healed and how far her and Cal's relationship has come. I'm happy for her, for them. Truly.

When she winds down, she coaxes me, "Now tell us about your new job."

I lean forward and murmur two words, "The Agency."

Libby's eyes flash with joy while Cal's flare with resignation. She exclaims, "Does that mean you'll be based here in DC?"

I relax back in my chair. "It does."

Cal mutters, "Great. Just great."

I burst into laughter. Annoying the crap out of Cal is just an added bonus to not being shot at as often as I used to be.

5

Present QUESTIONS

PARKER

"Then how did you and your wife meet?"

I can practically feel the warm ocean breeze caress my face. Just as Agent Fox opens her mouth to tell me to answer, I again try to narrow the scope of Fox's questions. "Look, yesterday was a long ass day. Can you skip the bullshit drain circling and just get to the questions you actually give a damn about?"

Her eyes narrow on my face. "That isn't how it works." What she leaves unsaid is, *and you know it.*

My lip curls. "Fine."

"I'll ask again, how did you and your wife meet?"

"Accidentally."

"Where did you and your wife meet?"

"At a Luke Bryan concert in Playa del Carmen, Mexico."

Pamola shakes her head. Fox sneers at me. "Want to try again?"

I release a beleaguered sigh. "Fine. It was while Brendan Blake was playing *at* the Luke Bryan concert in Playa del Carmen."

Fox turns to Pamola, who nods. "Truth."

She crosses her arms. "So, you like country music?"

"Yes."

"Is that why you were at the concert?"

This is where being me sucks. I answer truthfully, "No."

6

THIRTEEN YEARS AGO—AGE 20

In the PAST

Bethany

After Dr. Powell's last visit to our home, something changed in my father. He finally came home from the cruise where my mother died—albeit five years after they were supposed to return from their final destination. He sought out grief counseling for himself and family counseling for all of us, "But only if you want to." I encouraged Ellie, Abe, and Jordan to go, to repair as much of their relationship with my father as they could.

It wasn't until Ellie asked me, "What about you, Bethany?" I reluctantly gave in.

It floored me to find the family therapist my father had us seeing was Dr. Powell. My shock was palpable as I shook his hand. "Well, this is quite the surprise."

My father awkwardly explained, "I didn't trust anyone other than Bern with our private family matters, Bethany."

My heart softened at that, knowing Dr. Powell didn't use a single bit of what he'd overheard that day on my father's porch during the *Sea Force* anniversary special.

Now, standing on the deck of the balcony of the hotel suite my friends rented for Crash My Playa—a honey of an all-inclusive concert hosted by Luke Bryan in Playa del Carmen, Mexico that features not only country's favorite hottie, but Small Town Nights, Brendan Blake, and a load of others—a breeze cools off the sweltering air. Bodies shake along to the pumping music in the swimming pools three floors below, singing along to a Garth Brooks song amping up the crowd in between acts as the crew changes up the stage.

I have a clear shot from my balcony of all the action, including keeping an eye on my girlfriends, whom I met a few months ago when I transferred into Rice—girls who encouraged me to come to Mexico during our winter break.

Rice, one of my top three schools. A school I transferred into in September at both my father's and Dr. Powell's urging. Something I agreed to, providing I continued to work at McCallister Construction on long weekends and all breaks. That and, "You have to continue with therapy, Dad. Not for me, but for Ellie, Abe, and Jordan."

His eyes were bleak as he took hold of my hand. "Bethany, I don't plan on stopping it. And it's as much for you as for your brothers and sister."

"Dad..." My voice trailed off. I knew I wasn't the important one in this equation any longer.

My father spoke with a certainty that assured me he'd been thinking about his words for a long while. "Your mother would be ashamed of me, Bethany." That and what he said next shattered both my heart and my reservations. "I know a part of me died on that cruise, honey, but the part of your mother that lived didn't. That's you kids. I forgot that her heart lived on."

"I don't think you forgot," I whispered.

"What?" my father and Dr. Powell exclaimed.

That's when I admitted the most painful secret I'd been keeping back during therapy to that point, "Every time you look at me, I think you wish I wasn't here." I lifted my head and met my father's tormented eyes. "You wish Mama was."

"Bethany, is that how you really feel?" Dr. Powell questioned.

My eyes cut to his. "It's what I've lived."

My father broke down at the certainty in my words. Was it that moment we began to heal? I can't be certain. I just know that in the last twenty-four months, I finally felt comfortable leaving my family behind and being just a twenty-year-old woman.

Consequences, be damned.

Leaning against the balcony, I take a sip of the rum cocktail I mixed earlier and eagerly await Brendan Blake to take the stage. In the meanwhile, my hair lifts in the breeze as I stare out over the blue-green waters crashing against the sugar sand beach.

The first peace I've had in seven years is ruined when a voice barks at me, "Christ, no one up here is interested in you posing. Why don't you go join your little friends waving at you from the pool?"

I whip my head to the left and meet steel gray eyes boring into mine. The man, clad only in board shorts, has his back to the setting sun, giving me a perfect view of enormous muscles that are darkly tanned from the Mexican sun. I admire the breadth of his shoulders—a build I normally only find on the guys I work with on my father's construction sites.

Unfortunately, his attitude needs to be adjusted and it's too bad I left my tool kit back at home.

I find my eyes drifting up and down his form until they rest on his chiseled lips—lips set in a deep frown that just ruined my perfect beach oasis. My eyes narrow before I demand angrily, "What did you say?" I tip my head back and swallow another glug of my fruity drink, fortifying myself for his next words.

He lifts the bottle I didn't notice at his side before sneering, "Meow, meow, meow."

"Is that supposed to mean something?"

"No. It's what you girls sound like when you're all talking. Do any of you ever shut up?"

I shrug before answering him honestly. "I wouldn't know."

He rakes his eyes up and down over me before he slugs back another swallow. "Are you just like your friends?"

"What's that supposed to mean?" I grind out.

"Too busy fucking your latest toy to understand what the pounding on the other side of the wall means at four a.m.?"

I sneer at the bottle—catching sight of the rum label. I'm remembering the months of my father's drinking I endured, the insults hurled at me. I didn't survive being my mother's doppelgänger to deal with this stranger's abuse. "No."

"Just no?"

I expound upon my answer. "No is a full sentence."

"Yes."

"Also a full sentence. I'm impressed," I taunt.

He rolls his ridiculously attractive eyes, causing a tiny flutter in my stomach. I elucidate on my earlier dismissal. "Not that it's any of your business, but—"

"Honey, your friends made it my business when they screeched down my hotel room after they kicked their living vibrators out. That's before they held the world's longest monologue about what bikinis they planned on wearing today." He lifts the bottle to his lips again.

"It wasn't me."

"And I'd believe that because..."

"I missed the plane." I gesture my arm out to encompass the concertgoers. "You know the plane from Houston to here so I could be here on time?"

"Oh." He turns his back on me. Dismissing me because, why? I'm not some hapless being willing to indulge in his tantrum?

I think not.

A powerful kick of fury leaps into my veins. At least that's what I tell myself it is. I snap, "I missed the plane. They told me it would be okay and that they would pick me up at the airport. Do you see anyone else here?"

He snickers. "I could probably give you their damn itinerary if you want it."

At that moment, a screech can be heard as a cooler filled with water is dumped on top of the perfectly coiffed hair of some girls bouncing up and down in the pool. Seeing it happen to Naomi, I point in her direction before giggling. "I've got a good view right here. Thanks."

A reluctant grin crosses his face. He holds out a behemoth hand. "Thorn."

I take it and shake it firmly. "Bethany."

He gives me a head to toe perusal. "So, Bethany, what caused you to miss the plane?"

I shake my head. "I can't tell you."

"Oh, but, darlin', you really can. I know lots of secrets."

Thinking of the secured compartmentalized facility I was helping my father's crew outfit for a US government contractor for a small mint, I lean on the metal balustrade that separates our balconies and tease my neighbor, "If I told you, I'd have to kill you."

Something deep flashes in those silver eyes. "Well, well, well. We have something in common after all."

I hold myself perfectly still as he leans forward. When the alcohol blasts off his breath and almost knocks me off my feet, I gasp, "What's that?"

"That's my line."

It turns out laughter is a good repellent from alcohol fumes. Thorn leans back and winks before saying, "You're not as annoying as your roommates."

"Thanks. I think?"

Magnanimously, he offers, "Pull up a chair."

Still unable to pinpoint what makes me want to spend time with him instead of joining my friends, I accept his offer.

TWO HOURS LATER, Brendan Blake is wrapping up his set, crooning away his number one song, "Broken Boots," to the adoration of the crowd while Thorn and I proceed to get progressively more drunk. Well, at least I have. I'm not certain if Thorn's body build causes him to process alcohol differently. Regardless, his smooth as dark chocolate voice hasn't betrayed him a single time, whereas I hiccup every few seconds.

I've also told him all about me to the point he's cracked a joke, "Mata Hari, you're not."

Stifling a burp, I lift my drink to tap it against his bottle. "I still haven't told you what I do."

He ticks off, "College student by day. Construction worker by night. I'd ask if you dance in leg warmers in a strip club, but that would check off too many of my fantasies for one woman."

It takes me a minute, but then I whack him on his biceps for referencing *Flashdance*. "You think you're cute, Thorn."

His lips curl. "So, my mother's told me."

There was something about him that felt different. The way he'd been looking at me, the way his hand brushed mine as we stood close, overlooking the crush of people. It made my skin tingle with awareness. His silver, intense eyes held mine every time I opened my mouth to speak. It was like Thorn could see inside me, past every wall I'd built up.

Though I tried to act casual, my heart was racing. The more time we spent together tonight, the more I realized how much I was drawn to him. His confidence, his strength—even though it often came off as brash and overbearing—made me feel both intrigued and safe at the same time.

Something I haven't felt since long before my mother died.

"You okay?" His voice was low, barely audible over the music, but it sent shivers down my spine. He offers me the bottle, which I note still seems rather full in comparison to the number of drinks I've consumed, but I reject it with a violent shake of my head.

"No! I, uh...I don't eat or drink anything from strangers."

"Smart girl."

"You think so?"

"Yeah, B. I do."

"So, we're on a nickname basis?"

There's a pregnant pause before, "Why not?"

"Then what do I call you?"

His lips twist. "Thorn is my nickname."

Unusual but fitting. *He's as prickly as the thorns on Mama's roses.* The next thing I know, Thorn's head is tossed back with laughter. "Thank you, B. That's probably the nicest compliment I've ever received."

"I guess...you're welcome?"

He leans forward, a tiny smirk lingering on his lips. I lean forward and moisten mine. Because he's so close, the tip of my tongue grazes against his skin. It's salty due to sweat, masculine, and delicious.

Our breathing increases.

His eyes flick between my eyes and my mouth. Mine drift to half-mast as his paw of a hand slides up and around the nape of my neck. His other grips the balcony between us. Holding me in place, he murmurs, "Do you want me to kiss you, pretty little B?"

"Yes," comes my breathless moan just before Thorn's lips capture mine. The second they do, the sun is eclipsed and the pounding music is drowned out by the pounding of my heart. His tongue strokes over mine as he tangles the fingers of the hand holding my neck into my hair. When he angles his head, I tip mine for a better fit.

His utter maleness makes me feel more feminine than I ever have before. Then again, I've never met a man like Thorn before—a man who has made kissing a demand of all my senses. He tugs my lower lip into his mouth and begins a slow slaughtering of my defenses when he holds my eyes as he sucks my lip in and out.

Giving me an idea of other things he'd like to do.

Since I'm on board for whatever he has in mind, I wrap my arm around his neck, causing him to growl deep in his throat. Releasing the hold he has on my neck, he's about to haul me over the wrought iron bar when the door behind me flies open. "Bethany? Bethany McCallister? Where is your pretty little ass? Did you finally make it?" screeches my roommate, Lily.

The descent of Thorn's lips immediately stops. His eyes search mine before he chokes out, "Bethany...McCallister?" As if knowing my full name is a shock to him.

As if it isn't torturous to be me, especially when he pulls back and moves away as Lily makes her presence known by squealing. "Come on, babe! We have a perfect spot in the water right next to the stage."

I cut my eyes to the side, but Thorn's disappeared. I touch my lips, feeling the swollen bottom lip that was about to mimic the sex acts I was hoping would follow. Obviously, I can thank the men who took my mother's life for one more thing—making an attractive man who knows my story finding me repugnant once he hears my full name.

Asshole.

7

Present QUESTIONS

PARKER

"Then why were you in Playa del Carmen?"

Ahh, Fox is impressing me with her attempt at a run around the good old *Have you ever traveled to a foreign country? If so, what was the purpose of your visit?* question. My response is simple but effective. "That's classified."

Fox bursts out with, "That's bullshit."

I quirk a brow over at Deere, who is in charge of my medical bull-shit meter. He nods, indicating I'm telling the truth. Just then, the phone next to Pamola rings. Fox stomps over and snatches it up. She snaps, "What?" before her face pales significantly. "Yes, ma'am. I understand. Of course."

I can't help but wonder which member of my staff just ripped into Fox for sticking her nose where it didn't belong. Still, her line of questions brings me back to the afternoon I met Bethany on the balcony between our rooms, where Brendan Blake was singing, rum flowing—albeit not even as close for me as it was for my wife, and the tropical breeze surrounded us.

Regretfully, there was a reason I wasn't as close to intoxicated as she was. A reason I had to bail on her after the best first kiss of my life. And it had nothing to do with finding out my wife's full name.

In the PAST

PARKER

Stunned by discovering the identity of the outlandishly beautiful woman I just kissed, I'm infuriated when my Rolex vibrates with the signal I've been waiting for all day. Two short pulses followed by a long one. Shit. Still, even as I break the kiss, I verify, "Bethany McCallister?"

When she nods, my head spins at the irony of fate throwing Linc McCallister's daughter in my path. The SEAL motto floats through my mind. "The only easy day was yesterday." Obviously my predecessors who believed that never knew they'd be confronted by the daughter of past missions' ghosts.

Unfortunately, I have to leave her to her caterwauling friend and haul ass as my transpo is leaving downstairs in less than three minutes. Slinking away, as soon as I'm within the shadows of my room, I snatch up my go bag.

Still, I can't help but look back at the blond standing just where I left her.

Fuck.

THE MEXICAN SUN is quivering low on the horizon, casting long shadows as I crouch behind an abandoned building on the outskirts of Playa del Carmen. Sweat drips down my neck as the heat rises in waves, trying to suffocate me in my gear. But the discomfort caused by the heat isn't what has my nerves frayed.

It's remembering the look on Bethany's face as I turned around at the last second at the door.

One minute, I had her wrapped in my arms, feeling a connection I'd never felt before. Something real. All day I'd been enchanted by her laughter, the way her eyes lit up when she flirted with me. Then there was that kiss—that punch to the gut. A moment of time I never wanted to end, but then, it was gone. Snatched away by duty.

Adjusting my earpiece, I keep an eye on the small compound across the road. The worn structure blends seamlessly into the rundown neighborhood surrounding it. But the intel I was provided makes me know better. Inside, behind those crumbling walls, are two high-value targets—a cartel lieutenant and a computer filled with information on several arms deals of stolen US prototypes. That was why I was sent to Playa del Carmen in the first place. Why I had to leave without a warning or a goodbye to Bethany.

Certainly, I couldn't give her an explanation even if I did know the integrity her family possessed firsthand.

Lifting my sniper rifle, I peer through the night scope to see into the ramshackle building. Just then, a familiar voice comes through my earbud. My former SEAL teammate, Kyle, asks, "Thorn, do you have eyes on the target?"

"Yeah," I mutter, my voice low and steady. "Gutierrez is prepping for the meet."

"Hold position. We're two minutes out."

"Roger that."

I sit back on my heels, my mind wandering despite the adrenaline surging through my veins. This is the life I chose—a life of duty, patriotism, and protection. It was what I was trained for, what I was good at. But now I'm wondering how many more times I can walk away unscathed. How much time have I lost because I closed myself off?

I glance at my watch. Time is running out. I have to stay sharp, stay focused. The cartel is ruthless, and any mistake would be deadly —not just for me, but for my team and anyone else in the vicinity. There is no room for error, no space for my personal life to interfere.

My whole life has been like this. Secrets. Lies. The job. Having to compartmentalize. Never letting someone—save a select few—get too close. But tonight...felt different. Walking away from Bethany felt wrong. The look in her eyes as I left stayed with me when I normally could shove anyone or anything aside.

Damn it, I can't stop thinking about her. The way she'd looked at me just before I left—it was like I'd betrayed her, even though that couldn't be possible. She wasn't associated with the men inside this dump. Maybe it's because of who she is, but something inside me calls out for her approval.

Well, you ass, kissing and running probably wasn't the best way to get it, I mock myself. *But this is the life you choose to live.*

I hear Kyle murmur in my ear again. "Thorn, we're in position. Green light. Move in on my mark."

"Copy that," I reply, forcing myself into mission mode.

I can't afford to think about anything but the mission right now. Not when I am about to provide backup for a situation that could go tits up any second. But as I ready my weapon and peer through the scope to support the primary team, a small part of me wonders if I'll ever have the chance to make things right with her.

9

Present QUESTIONS

PARKER

"It's nice to know you aren't just a cretin to your employees."

I glare up at Fox for an uncomfortably long minute—for her—before I unexpectedly admit, "I started young."

"Yet, you had a solid home life."

"Like I said, it was difficult for me after my parents died."

"Was that before or after the events aboard the *Sea Force*?"

I know we're about to get into some questions that may make the people on the other side of the glass antsy, even though the events took place almost twelve years ago. "After. Long after."

"Are they the reason you left black ops?"

"Yes."

"They died in a car crash?"

"Yes."

"What happened?"

"They were leaving my home. A semi-truck driver fell asleep at the wheel."

"I'm sorry for your loss." Fox's voice is almost a rote platitude.

"I'm sorry for our nation's loss," I snap, irritated that this agent didn't do her damn homework before coming in to interrogate me.

Deere murmurs, "Fox. Vitals."

Fox notes my chest rising and falling, my fury palpable. Her heels snapping against the concrete floor, she makes her way over to Pamola's desk before flipping to the front dossier in my massive file.

It's then, and only then she whispers, "Yes, sir. It was a great loss for our country."

10

In the PAST

PARKER

The rigamarole of the pomp and ceremony I've had to endure, from permitting my father's desk to be dropped in black crepe to delegations of corrupt cocksuckers coming to pay their respects, is about to do me in. The only thing that caught me in the gut was seeing the flag flown at half-mast and knowing it was meant for him, them.

That's when the insidious pain started crawling through every pore of my body. I was unable to escape it as I wandered through my childhood home in Virginia Beach as I stared at meticulously framed photos of the three of us from when I was a baby through my growing years. Tears streamed down my face at the pride evident on theirs when I graduated from the Academy and then the image of me they took when my commander pinned on my trident after I earned my Navy Special Warfare Operator rating.

Moving down the row of photos, I touched one my mother had framed of us after I returned from my mission down in Mexico, where I was trying to recruit college students in border schools to work for the Agency to help stop drug cartels.

When I met *her*.

Shoving Bethany McCallister to the back of my mind, I took the picture off the wall and stared at the smirk on my father's face—a twist of the lips I inherited. My mother's silver eyes twinkle up at me from the two-dimensional image capturing the love and laughter I had until just a few short weeks ago.

Is this what you felt after you lost your mother on the Sea Force, Bethany McCallister? The rogue thought races through my head and I shove it back—way back—because right now, I can't unpack what happened that night in Mexico. Why I started talking to her.

More importantly, why I stopped.

The only thing I can think about is my parents are gone, and I'll never have another chance to tell them I love them.

GRIEF IS A CONSTANT COMPANION. If I had my way, I'd force every reporter trying to flash a camera in my face as I exit the back of the limousine carrying me to their gravesite to jump in the hole waiting to lower their caskets into the ground. I don't care that my father was Senator Albert Thornton—senior senator on the Senate Appropriations Committee, or that my mother, Lorraine Parker Thornton, was a well-respected pediatrician. Right now, all I care about is they're gone.

In my full dress uniform, with my trident pin gleaming on my front left breast, I make my way to the viewing area. I note that in addition to the paps, there are more people than just the leeches my father worked with. Some of my former team members have made it and—I'm so grateful—friends, including Cal and Libby.

Maybe, just maybe, I can make it through everything I have to do today as a son, a former SEAL, and as the face to the nation.

I stand at the edge of the gravesite, my fists clenched so tight that my nails dig into my palms, but I don't care. I can't feel anything except the gnawing emptiness in my chest and the weight of my broken heart.

The honor guard waiting to honor my father stands at rest in formation, rifles held at their sides, ready to send my father off—and my mother along with him. One flag-draped coffin, one draped in roses, both centered beneath the tent, looked surreal. There was no way they could hold the love, confidence, and memories my parents had bestowed upon me. My gloved fists clenched at my side. Especially when none of it made any sense.

As a SEAL, I had buried brothers, men I fought alongside. But this... burying my parents? The man who taught me to stand tall, to face the world head on? The mother who reminded me every time I came home from a mission I still have a heart? This was different. This was unbearable.

The priest's voice echoes through the quiet crowd, reciting prayers, but I don't hear a word. I stare at the coffins, my mind replaying every life lesson, every stupid teenage argument. My first tear falls.

Then I recall how my father would clasp me to him each and every time I strode through the front door after every mission, the way I'd scoop up my mother right after. Now, I know why those moments were so precious. It was because I wasn't just feeling their love more in those moments; I also felt their relief in my safe return.

How foolish was I to take theirs for granted?

I blink against the sun, the glare bouncing off the polished wood of the casket. My jaw tightened as I forced the memories away. I'm angry. No, more than angry. Not at them, but at the whole damn situation. At how a man who was once a combat veteran, who survived war zones and firefights, who'd made it through some of the most dangerous missions imaginable, had been taken out by something as mundane as a car accident. It's a goddamn irony that I can't swallow.

As the final words of the eulogy fade, the honor guard steps forward, the rifles snapping into position. I flinch at the sound of the gunfire—each volley echoing across the quiet cemetery, each crack of the rifles driving home the reality of what is happening.

The honor guard folds the flag with precise, practiced movements until they finally hand it to me. I don't want it. I want my family back. I want them alive. I want to tell everyone to go the fuck away so I can release the sounds desperate to escape from the depths of my soul. But I bury that deep, take the flag, gripping it like it is the last piece of them I have left.

I look down at the flag in my hands, my gloved fingers catching on the folds in the fabric.

Eventually, people start to leave, murmuring their condolences as they pass. I barely hear them. I don't want their sympathy. I don't want their words. I just want them back. "Thorn," is said softly in a sweetly southern voice, accompanied by a heavy hand on my shoulder.

My head twists to the side only to find a concerned Libby and Cal. Somewhere in my numbness, I'm only mildly surprised to find Libby's cousin Sam Akin and his wife, Iris, directly behind them. I never even noticed them in the crowd. I am physically unable to do anything but stare at my parent's coffins. My voice cracks as I manage to force out, "Thank you all for coming."

Cal's hand comes down on my shoulder. "Let us know if you need anything, man. We're here for you."

Eventually, everyone left—including the media. I don't know how long it took. I do know I watched as the undertakers dug their graves, the wind carrying the scent of freshly dug earth.

Finally, it is just me, alone in front of the grave. I look down at the flag in my hands again, and I can't stop the tears this time. They fall, hot and heavy, as I sink to my knees beside the freshly dug graves.

I stay there until the caskets are lowered, my head bowed, my shoulders shaking.

Finally, I reach out and pluck two perfect red roses from the arrangement that blankets my mother's casket. Kissing each one, I fling them on top of their coffins. "I love you both. I always will."

That's when I decide, if love is going to cause this much hurt, I never want to feel it again.

Ever.

11

Present QUESTIONS

PARKER

"Do you have any friends or family members involved in organizations that oppose US interests?"

I drawl laconically, "I have friends and family who oppose my best interests. You'd have to ask them if they've joined any organizations. I do know they meet together on frequent social occasions."

By now, Fox has either plotted my murder or is enjoying my daring as I reply to her no-nonsense questions with my trademark sarcasm. I'm not quite certain, but I'd bet my left nut Pamola had to stifle a chuckle over that last comment. Still, Fox perseveres. "Are you certain?"

My sigh is drawn out. "Listen, I'm not exactly the poster boy they use to advertise *Bumble BFF*, okay?"

"I'm impressed you know what *Bumble BFF* is, sir."

"I have friends with kids. I need to know exactly how to ruin their lives."

"Now that sounds a lot more like you."

"It does, doesn't it?"

"So, if you didn't meet your wife on social media, how did you two reconnect after so long?"

"Sheer happenstance."

Fox's eyes cut to Pamola, who confirms I'm again telling the truth. Her jaw falls open a bit. "Really?"

"Yes." I sometimes wonder what would have happened if I had decided not to annoy the crap out of Cal by attending a party thrown by Libby. But I'll be forever grateful to the annoying prick that I did.

12
ELEVEN YEARS AGO—AGE 23

In the PAST

Bethany

My back is literally against the wall and I fervently wish I was anywhere but here. Despite my desire to knock back a few drinks and escape, a promise is a promise.

And I promised. It makes my heart sick to think about all the promises that have been broken in my life, leaving me with no choice but to keep my own when I make them. So, I've become a new pillar supporting the wall in Libby Sullivan's home. I'm not just obligated to celebrate the expansion of her design business, Deja Vu, as one of her friends but as her work colleague since, according to her, "If it wasn't for your incredible construction skills, B, I'd never have been able to put Deja Vu on the map."

I countered her claim, but my business lines have been ringing off the hook since Libby gave me a shout-out during her acceptance speech when Deja Vu won the Pinnacle Award at the Premier Design Awards last month.

Libby's husband, Cal, saunters up next to me. I'm about to collapse against him and beg him not to leave me in this sea of strangers that have invaded their home, but that's before he opens his mouth—a mouth Libby has stressed on more than one occasion speaks before it thinks. "I almost didn't recognize you, Bethany."

"Why not?"

"A dress? Heels?" He leans closer. "Is there someone you're trying to impress? Come on, you can let me know. I keep secrets for a living."

Even knowing he's telling the truth about his profession, I still hiss, "It's your wife's fault. She banned my usual go-to wardrobe."

He throws his head back, laughing uproariously. "Like I didn't know that? According to Libby, the night at the Pinnacle Awards was the first time she's ever seen you not in jeans."

I bristle. "And the problem with that is?"

He holds his hands up before backing up a step as if in surrender. "None."

I tug at the hem of my black cocktail dress, somehow hoping that might stretch the material a few more inches closer to my knee than the V between my legs. Yeah. No such luck. I release a sigh before admitting, "Until last month, I didn't own anything more formal than jeans and boots."

For some reason, that causes Cal's face to soften. Slinging an arm around my shoulders, he guides me away from the wall. I immediately stumble in the asinine heels the store clerk gushed to me, "Are simply perfect with your dress."

She obviously hadn't tried to walk in them more than the six feet I had to ascertain their comfort or she'd have realized my idea of Doc Martens was a safer choice with the short black beaded number I was already self-conscious about.

Fortunately, Cal's arm around my shoulders kept me upright even as he jokes, "Would a drink help correct those balance issues, B?"

I give it serious consideration for a moment before asking, "With my social awkwardness or my balance issues?"

"Either. Both." To his credit, he tries to suppress the smirk that wants to spread across his handsome face.

I grumble, "I bet Libby doesn't have these problems."

"Wanna bet?"

My eyes widen as he stops a passing waiter to snag a glass of champagne, which he presses into my hand. He confides, "She'd much rather be barefoot in jeans running after the kids at our family home near Charleston."

Recalling everything I was ever told about Elizabeth Akin Sullivan before I ever met her, I'm flabbergasted. Taking a moment to reconcile Cal's Libby with the woman I heard stories about over the years, long before I met her—I take a cautious sip and scrunch my nose as the fizziness of the champagne worms its way into my sinus cavity. I sneer, "People pay good money to drink this?"

Cal's eyes crinkle in the corner. I'm just waiting for him to make some kind of smart ass remark which might end up with him wearing the rest of these bubbles when his eyes narrow at something just beyond my shoulder. Before I can spin around in my stiletto death traps to see what's wrong, his lips press together in a tight line before he grits out an almost tangible unwelcome, "Thorn."

No. It can't be. There has to be two men in this world with the same nickname. But Lady Luck, who has never been on my side, shows me I'm one of her least favorite people in the world because I hear a voice I never expected to hear again in my life—a voice whose very essence slithers through my body, melting away my well-erected barriers the way warm dark chocolate melts cold ice cream. "Cal. Quite the party. Where's the woman of the hour?"

Cal waves his free arm in a vague circle. "Around. But it's women of the hour."

"Oh?"

I recall from that day spent in Mexico, Thorn is generally a man of few words. Unbidden, the way I met him surges to the forefront of my mind. The warmth of the Mexican sun, the burn of rum, the surge of desire from our kiss. I put an immediate stop to my thoughts. Stop. *You met him when you were trying to escape, having just been freed from your prison of raising your brothers and sister after your father's shell returned without your mother from their anniversary cruise. You met Thorn trying to celebrate being on your own and not feeling the pressure of keeping your father's company afloat. Our worlds intersected for a simple heartbeat until he turned tail and ran when he realized who you are.*

Then, like the chicken shit he was—is?—he ran away.

I'm stiff as a board beneath Cal's draped arm, facing partially away when Thorn growls, "Did Libby get a dye job, or are you into blonds now?"

"Fuck you, Thorn. This is one of her friends." Cal squeezes my shoulder as if to reassure me not to be offended by Thorn's words. *Don't worry, Cal. I'm used to his obnoxious behavior.*

My head twists away. In my head, I plead silently for him not to introduce us.

She listens to me for once. But the cowardly lion, as I choose to remember Thorn so I don't fall into the occasional thoughts of "what if?" after that scorching kiss, just can't let it drop. He steps closer to both of us. Shoving out his hand, his thick fingers, which I remember all too well tangled in my hair, he introduces himself. "Parker Thornton."

"Thorn and I knew each other when he was a SEAL before I worked for Hudson Investigations," Cal explains.

I can't help but be impressed. A SEAL. That explains the cockiness, the arrogance he displayed in our one afternoon together. What it doesn't explain is why he was such a dick finding out my identity.

Turning my head, I meet Thorn's eyes. My lips purse as his

silvery orbs are eclipsed by the pupils once he recognizes me. His lips lift in a smile. "Bethany."

Twisting a little so I face Cal, I drawl, "I've had the pleasure once of meeting Thorn. Spare me a second."

"Bethany, we should talk." Thorn rumbles.

Ignoring that deep voice, I inform my host, "I think I'll go find Libby. We have a lot to celebrate tonight."

Cal's doing his best to not bust a gut laughing if the persistent lip twitch and chest heaves are any indicators. He scans the room before informing me, "I see her in the sunroom holding court with Keene and Ali."

Ensuring I'm steady on my heels, I make my way in that direction. Thorn reaches out and grips my elbow. "Let me walk you over. We'll...talk."

My eyes drift down to his fingers on my bare skin before I jut my chin pugnaciously and bite out, "What would we have to talk about, Thorn? How you heard my full name after kissing me and then walked out without a word?"

Cal lets out a low whistle. "Wow. And to think I attributed some brains to you."

"Not now, Cal," he grits out.

"Don't worry, Cal. It's more like not ever," I reassure him.

Thorn's jaw locks. Perversely, I give myself a mental pat on the back. I guess not many women have turned down meeting Parker Thornton, former Navy SEAL. "Excuse me."

With that, I carefully pick my way over to Libby's side of the room. When I get there, a raucous cheer goes up. Libby hands me a glass of fresh champagne before announcing to the room at large, "Bethany McCallister, everyone! Architect and lead contractor of Hudson Investigations, DC's new office! The reason we were awarded the Pinnacle Award."

Lifting my glass, I toast her back. "Libby Sullivan, whose vision of what Hudson Investigations should be here in DC made it easy." As applause breaks out around us, my eyes meet Thorn's across the room. Something flips low in my stomach when I realize his gaze is intent on me.

It causes me to tingle, remembering that kiss.

With a small amount of regret, I turn my back on him, effectively shutting my mind down from trying to build a bridge between my past and my present. I just know if I invite Thorn in, I'll never be the same.

13

ELEVEN YEARS AGO—AGE 33

Present QUESTIONS

PARKER

"Now I'm going to ask you that significant life event question. How on earth did you convince your wife to ever go on a date with you?" Fox taunts me.

I glare at her as Deere and Pamola stifle laughter as best they can. "I can be charming." When I want to be. For my wife, I really wanted to be.

"Sir, no offense, but I have no qualms about the fact you're lying. In fact, I'm not even considering this a lie. It's more along the lines of delusional behavior."

"Actually, Fox," Pamola starts.

She groans. "Don't say it."

My lips quirk. I don't speak a word because Pamola does it for me. "Not kidding. He's not."

"How? You're sanctimonious, smug, overly superior—"

"You list those qualities like they're bad things."

Deere pipes up, "I just want details. I mean, has anyone actually ever heard the story?"

A gleam appears in Fox's eyes. She flips through my file and I groan inwardly, knowing the answer already. No. No one knows how I managed to convince Bethany to go out with me.

I became her little bitch, supplicating myself to her every whim. I begged. I pleaded.

Ultimately, it took an act worse than any other I've ever done for my country.

I went bowling.

14

In the PAST

PARKER

I f anyone ever knew what I did, my clearance might get docked.

I could lose my job.

I might be sent away by the Agency to some post in Timbuktu—yeah, no. That wasn't happening. I'd just quit and go work somewhere else. Still, I'm uncomfortable with what I've done to the point I'm shifting in my Saville Row suit outside what looks like the entrance to a dive bar, all so I could "run into" Bethany. But what has me doing the fire ant dance in my pants is how I got the intel to be here.

I couldn't convince Libby or Cal to tell me anything about her beyond confirming what I heard yelled at their home a few nights ago. Bethany McCallister led the construction team behind Deja

Vu's build out of Hudson Investigation's new office in DC. It wasn't her father, Linc, a man I've actually met.

It is the blond sprite who has been living in my dreams since that kiss on the balcony in Mexico. I never thought our lives would intersect again, which is why I never looked before.

I did today. I did the unethical. Something I'll have to report on my next clearance re-up. I used my Agency credentials to track Bethany to where she is right now—just beyond the doors inside Spare Tavern. According to her cell pings, she comes here at least once a week for several hours, so I brace myself before going in.

I hadn't planned on coming to her weekly bowling match. In fact, bowling wasn't my thing. But the moment I heard from one of my analysts that this was where she went every Friday night with her crew, I couldn't shake the idea. Call me persistent, but I wasn't going to let our reconnection—as awkward as that meeting was at that party—be the end of whatever this could be between us. If it even is anything. At this point, I'm not even sure where this may go, but I know I want to find out.

My shoulders droop imperceptibly as I make my way to the door. She doesn't owe me a damn thing, but I hope she'll hear me out. When I realized Bethany has a clearance of her own—a clearance level definitely lower than mine but not too shabby—I realized I could let her in on why I had no choice but to leave.

Why I can make the choice now to stay—if she's amenable to spending time with me. To seeing where these—*god, are these emotions? No wonder people fuck up all the time over them*, I think, disgusted. I yank open the door, anxious to get a drink in my hand so I can numb them slightly.

But the moment I cross over into Spare Tavern, my mind blanks except for one single thought. *They must have superior soundproofing.*

The cottage-esque exterior is a superior camouflage for what lies in the heart of Spare Tavern. Over and over, as I absorb the trap I just walked into, lightning cracks over and over. In reality, it's the sound of resin striking wood in the lanes just below the upper landing I'm standing on.

The sound hit me first—the loud crack of bowling balls smashing into pins, the hum of laughter, and the occasional groan of defeat—whether that's because they missed a critical ball or guttered it entirely. I'm frozen in place temporarily, shock over the wall-to-wall people embracing a tried and true American tradition.

All those years I spent fighting in hell holes around the world, and I never realized until right now, I did it for this—for the first date, I clocked at twelve o'clock. For the family birthday party over in lane six. For the league of at least semi-pro players in matching attire, and, though I didn't spot her right away, a group that I instantly knew were her people. Construction workers. Big, loud, covered in tattoos and paint splatters, probably as comfortable in steel-toed boots as I was in a tailored suit.

Then I see her amid the burly men in lane eight, and the world fades away.

Leaning casually against the scorer's table, holding a beer, her blond hair in a messy ponytail and a worn baseball cap pulled low over her brow, she looks like she belongs here, with those rough and tumble workers, like she'd never felt out of place a day in her life whereas I'm using deep breathing exercises to propel myself toward the stairs toward her.

That's when a voice shouts near my ear above the din. "Hey, mister?"

"Yeah?"

"Are you planning on going down below?"

Not losing Bethany in my sights, my chest aches. She leaps in the air after a particularly impressive roll of the ball. Having never been bowling, I know back slaps and the military. But this? I'm completely out of my league.

I give an imperceptible tip of my head, whereupon the kid says, "Then we need to get you shoes."

I glance down at my Church's dress loafers and raise a brow. "These shoes are perfectly fine, thank you."

The kid's lips split, revealing a wide line of braces. "Not for the alley, mister."

"Ahh, you have a uniform."

"Yeah, whatever. What size?"

"A twelve should work." Then I watch in fascination as the kid plunks a pair of shoes on the counter and sprays them with disinfectant. I blurt out my thoughts before I can hold them back, "You voluntarily do this?" Revulsion drips in every word.

He snorts. "What reason do you think I'd risk inhaling stank feet?"

Fair point. "It's a paycheck."

"Got it in one." He then asks if I need a lane. I point to Bethany's, where she and her friends seem to be wrapping up their game. I mention I'll be heading that way and, to my pleasure and dismay, am told, "No problem." I make a mental note to assign guards to Bethany starting next week. She's too unprotected.

Too vulnerable.

After taking my card, I'm handed my shoes, given a sheet of paper on how to hook up to the WiFi—no fucking way. I can see some pimple-faced ass hat trying to hack my phone and realizing I'm the mother-fucking associate director of the Agency. Then I'll be fending off attacks all night instead of focusing on the woman I can't seem to stop obsessing about.

Before I know it, I'm behind the hard plastic chairs near to Bethany just as she's about to bowl again. I admire her trim physique as she takes three steps forward, swings her arm back, and crouches down, pulling her jeans tight against her ass. An ass, I remember lasciviously, which fit perfectly in my big hands. Hands that wanted so fucking badly to explore every inch of her perfect skin. That was until I was dragged away from her for my damn mission and my patriotic duty.

I swallow, the memory of our conversation at Cal and Libby's party smashing through my memories of our day together in Playa Del Carmen. She barely acknowledged me—probably thought I'd forgotten her. And to be fair, I'd given her that impression. I'd been pulled into an op that night that kept me out of the country. Then, after my parents' funeral, I elected to leave for the better part of eighteen months until I was shot and sidelined. *But she doesn't know that,* the insidious voice inside my head reminds me. Determined to have a long overdue conversation with her, I promise myself nothing's dragging me away tonight unless Bethany plans on doing the dragging.

As she's doing her celebratory dance, she spots me. Happiness seems to dissipate into thin air as Bethany storms up to me. She snaps, "What are you doing here, Thorn?"

I rub the back of my neck. "I guess I wanted a chance to see you again. After all, seeing you for the first time at Cal and Libby's the other night didn't go so well."

Something shifts and moves behind her eyes. I recognize her stifling her curiosity before she says, "How did you know I would be here?"

I step closer, not just so we're not overheard but so I can determine if our time in Mexico was a fluke. *Judging by the way my cock leaps to attention after it presses against the trousers of my suit, I'd say not,* I think sardonically. Without thought or repercussion, I answer, "I tracked you."

Her eyes narrow. "How?"

I open my mouth to answer until I take in how pissed off she is. I decide to make her a bargain. "How about we play a game? If I win, I get to take you out." I sound a lot more confident than I really am.

"And if I do?" she asks suspiciously.

"Then you can ask me any question."

"Including how you tracked me?"

"Including that," I immediately agree.

Her lips twitch into a smile. With a flick of her long hair, she goes over and programs our names into the computer. Thorn. B. "Game on, Thorn."

"May the best person win, B."

God, please give me a miracle and let that be me.

BETHANY TAKES HER TURN, her movements fluid and effortless as she launches the ball down the lane. It crashes into the pins, sending all ten scattering in a perfect strike. Her friends whoop and cheer, and she turns back to me with a cocky grin.

"Top that," she teases, her eyes sparkling with mischief.

"Not sure I can."

Bethany studies me for a second, and I can see the gears turning in her head. "You don't exactly look like the bowling type, you know that, right?"

I look down at myself—down to the shirtsleeves in my suit. Definitely a more relaxed version of my usual office impeccability, but still, "I can adapt," I say, holding my hands up. "I'm flexible."

She snorts a laugh, and I take it as a small victory.

"Well, if you're flexible, then grab a ball, businessman. We're just about to start another round."

But the whole time, I know there is one thing I haven't told her—one thing that might push her away again if she finds out. My job. My life as a businessman isn't exactly the typical nine-to-five she probably imagined. And I am not sure how she'll take it once she knows the truth about what I do and who I work with.

I've learned over the years that people knowing I work at the Agency has the power to make them swoon with the desire to learn the most delicious *on dit* or scare them to death that their secrets will be exposed. *Where will Bethany fall once she finds out?* I wonder.

And she will ask since she's kicking my ass.

As the night winds down and the others start to pack up, Bethany and I end up sitting at a small table near the snack bar, finishing off our drinks. She leans back in her chair, her gaze flicking to me like she is sizing me up again.

"So, how did you find me?" She takes a pull from her bottle.

"I tracked you." Blunt, open.

Her head turns to the side to avoid spraying my suit. "Are you for real right now?"

I shrug. "Why lie? I wanted to see you again, but Cal and Libs were no help."

"That's borderline stalkerish, Thorn."

"I didn't use some crazy app, B. I typed your name into a computer and it spit out a whole plethora of data."

Her brows furrow as her gaze roams my face.

"You're a mystery, you know that?" she says, her voice low.

I raise an eyebrow. "Am I?"

She nods. "You're not a businessman, are you?"

"No."

"Nor are you a politician."

"Not even close." My voice catches at the end. I'm not certain with the noise in the alley she'd notice but surprisingly, her hand comes to rest on top of mine.

"I'm truly sorry to have read about your parents, Parker." The organ in the center of my chest flips around at her use of my first name for the first time as blood rushes back to it. Her fingers squeeze mine before she begins to withdraw. "I know what it feels like to lose one parent. Hell, for five years, I knew what it was like to lose both of them."

I flip my hand around so I prevent her from pulling away. "I want to get something out between us. Something I need for you to understand."

"O-okay?"

"I didn't leave that day because you're Bethany McCalister," I inform her bluntly, sizing up her reaction.

It doesn't take long for her to have one. Her expression closes down, and all empathy washes away by a mask of protection. "Then why did you leave?"

"I received a message. I had to go."

She scoffs. "Right."

"B, I'm not lying to you. I *had* to go."

"How did you receive the message?"

I lift my wrist and show her my Rolex. "There's a transmitter inside that emits a pulse. I had to leave *then* so things didn't FUBAR."

"Thorn?"

"Yes?"

"What do you even do, really?"

I hesitate, my heart thudding in my chest. This is it. The moment to be honest. But how much can I say? "I work in...troubleshooting," I say carefully, which is true enough. "It's complicated."

"Troubleshooting?" she repeats, clearly not buying it.

I exhale. "It's hard to explain, but I'll tell you more when we're in the right location."

Her eyes narrow slightly. "Right."

I can't blame her for being suspicious. I am asking her to trust me without giving her the full story. But I want to earn that trust, even if it takes time.

"I'm not trying to hide anything," I say. "Just..."

That's when she smiles and beckons me forward, a hint of mischievousness crossing her face. Cupping my ear, she whispers, "This is the kind of conversation we need to have inside one of my SCIFs. Isn't it Thorn?"

I had no way of knowing then, but her tacit understanding of who I am would seal our fate. Lifting her hand to my lips, I kiss the inside of her wrist. It's the same spot I did the day we were in Mexico together. Letting my lips linger as I stare into her fathomless blue eyes, I murmur, "Yeah, it is."

Her breath shudders out, whether due to my ministrations or my words, I'm not certain. "Well, at least this time, I'm going into this with my eyes wide open."

15

Present QUESTIONS

PARKER

"Pillow talk between you and your wife must be interesting."

At this, a devious smile twitches for just a second before I assume my serious mien. "Fox, you're not cleared to hear the pillow talk between me and my wife."

"So you admit there is some?" She's surprised. As with most polygraphs, most people deny pillow talk.

I shrug. "Why would I deny it?"

Even Pamola and Deere's jaws are slack as I—appear—to admit the cardinal sin of anyone with a national security clearance—discussing job specifics with one's spouse. The thing is, I'm not admitting to shit. Not caring two shits about their assumptions, I ask, "Would you like to hear about my wife's father's upcoming visit? Or maybe about how we're contemplating buying a second home in Texas?"

Fox's eyes narrow. "You know full well that's not the kind of pillow talk we're talking about."

My eyebrows skyrocket. "I'm not certain if you're allowed to ask me *those* kinds of questions, Fox."

At that, Pamola and Deere can't hold back their snickers. Despite getting hit with a glare hot enough to fry an egg, I continue on blithely, "I mean, we might be a decade or so older than you, but we've still..."

"Stop!" Fox shouts. "Just answer my question."

"Which was?"

"Do you discuss your job with your wife?"

"Generally."

"What about specifically?"

"You do know my wife is cleared at a very high level," I remind her.

"And do you discuss specifics about missions? Anything that would put American lives at risk?" she persists.

My jaw locks. "My wife runs a successful contracting firm to build facilities that are safe for you to do your job and for me to do mine. There are few times when our jobs intersect. That being said, she's my wife. She can damn well ask me if I'm okay, and she knows me well enough, has lived through enough, and is fucking smart enough to know if something is reported on the news, I've likely had my hand in it. But to answer your question explicitly, no. The only pillow talk we engage in is the kind that hopefully ends with my mouth on hers."

16

In the PAST

Bethany

When Parker said he wanted to cook for me about three months into our relationship, I'd thought he was joking. He was admittedly as much of a takeout eater as I was considering what he did.

I still can't believe I'm dating the associate director of the Agency. I mean, not only can he find out what I ate for breakfast—or even if I ate at all—simply by dialing up one of the satellites at his fingertips, he admitted his job isn't just troubleshooting one day when he stopped by and the Defense Intelligence Agency practically bowed to him as my latest SCIF was being certified.

"I'm an associate director of the Agency," he admitted when we were inside the vault that was buried in the basement of an otherwise normal office building on the outskirts of Reston, Virginia.

Floored by the knowledge, one thing I knew for certain was I couldn't inflate his already massive ego. Instead, I clapped my hands together and bounced up and down like a schoolgirl. "Ooh. Do they have you in charge of HR?"

In the short time we've been dating, I've learned Parker "Thorn" Thornton might have a lot going for him. He takes in the big picture. He doesn't make any decisions without all the information. He's loyal, which is fantastic when you're the one he's loyal to. One of the things he is not is patient. At all.

Add his ridiculous handsomeness, I can't help but be a little intimidated by him. It's nice to have the occasional imperfection to tease him about. And it is teasing. I could never intentionally hurt Parker. With every spare minute we've spent together, we're weaving ourselves more and more into one another's lives. We've spent time with Cal and Libby and their newborn. He's joined me for more Friday night bowling and I attended an Agency gala with him.

No, I wouldn't trade this overbearing, over-confident, confident man for anyone else on the planet.

Still, despite some heated kisses where, with the cold lingering in DC, I'm transported to the tropics each and every time his lips make a meal of mine, I want more. Tonight's invitation to dinner had me slipping on lace beneath my usual jeans and shirt. After all, his invitation is the kind of thing a man says to a woman when either he's trying to impress her or seduce her.

God, I hope it's the second.

But no—apparently, Parker is serious and wants something other than me on the menu. Now I stand in the middle of his sleek, modern kitchen, surrounded by enough stainless steel appliances to stock a professional chef's dream, I wonder if the way my thong's wedged between my ass cheeks in these jeans was worth it.

"I wasn't expecting this." I gesture to the kitchen as I take it in. It's all shiny and perfect— like it belongs as a feature in *Food Network*

Magazine belonging to Bobby Flay or some other professional. Still, for as sleek as the kitchen is, Parker looks slightly disheveled in his casual button-down shirt—sleeves rolled up, apron tied over his jeans.

He's holding his spatula like it's all he has to disarm an army of hostile invaders instead of its intended use to scrape the bottom of the non-stick pan. His usually cocky arrogance has taken a hit, and I can tell he is nervous. Then again, I could determine that intel from the war of clam sauce flung in a perimeter around him. "I, uh, thought I'd go all out," he says, a crooked grin on his face. "Figured a simple dinner wouldn't cut it."

I prop my chin on my hand while I sip my glass of wine, wondering how many people don't get to see past the cold shell he erects to the man beneath. Studying him while he frantically turns back to the stove in an attempt to save our dinner, I can't help but think how adorable he is in spite of my urge to laugh. Seeing the great Parker Thornton, super spook extraordinaire, be drowned under the troubled water of fettuccini is oddly endearing. "I'm impressed. What's on the menu, Chef?"

"Well..." He hesitates, glancing over his shoulder at the stove before he tosses the spatula into the sink with perfect precision. "I may have... miscalculated a few things."

I slide off my stool and make my way to him. Peering over at the pot, I see the glob of what was supposed to be pasta. In the next one is a grayish goop that definitely doesn't look delicious. Instead of making me want to swipe my finger through it, it bubbles ominously. "Miscalculated?"

"Yeah," he mutters, turning back to face me. "The sauce was supposed to simmer, but it's more like... boiling. And the pasta got a little, uh, goopy. Let's not talk about the bread."

I glance at the oven, where he marches over to pull out a tray of what used to be garlic bread. The edges are blackened, and I stifle a laugh.

"Okay, so it's a little overdone," I say, trying to hide my amusement.

Thorn lets out a sigh, wiping his hand across his forehead dramatically. "You're being nice. It's a disaster."

I shake my head as I relax against the counter. "It's not a disaster. It's... charming."

"Charming?" He raises an eyebrow. "So, burnt bread is your thing?"

"No, but a guy who tries really hard to impress me? Definitely my thing."

He flashes a wicked smile at me for that, his shoulders relaxing a little, though I can still see the tension in his jaw. "Well, I wanted tonight to be perfect. I wanted to do something that'd show you I'm not the douche who ghosted you in Mexico."

I walk over and gently tug at the apron he wrapped around his waist. "And you thought poisoning me was the way to go?"

He laughs, running a hand through his hair, his silver eyes sparkling with amusement. "Clearly, I need more practice."

Catching the familiar scent of his cologne, my head spins headily. "Look, you don't need to pull off some elaborate dinner to impress me. The fact that you even tried... that's what matters. Trust me, I've seen worse."

"Worse than this?"

"Way worse," I say, smirking. "You should see some of the meals I've thrown together on the job site."

His expression is clearly skeptical, as if he isn't sure whether to believe me. Then he grins again, shaking his head. "Okay, fair enough. But I still wanted to make tonight special."

"It is," I say, resting a hand on his arm. "It's special because it's you. Because you let me see you like this—messy, unsure, and human. It's kind of refreshing."

He meets my eyes, and for a second, I see something soft there, something vulnerable. It is a side of him I rarely get to see, and I like it. A lot.

"I'm not usually good at this kind of thing," he admits quietly, his gaze dropping to the floor. "Romantic gestures and all that."

"Well, you're doing fine so far."

A faint smile tugs at his lips. "You sure? Because I can still order pizza."

I wrap my arms around his waist. "Pizza sounds perfect."

The awkwardness melts away, and he lets out a deep breath. "Thank God. I thought I was going to have to eat my own cooking."

Still grinning, I tease him gently. "You could always keep the bread. By tomorrow, it should be hard enough to set it as a doorstop or something."

"Or a paperweight," he suggests, his grin widening. "Maybe I'll give it to you as a souvenir of the night."

I roll my eyes but can't help laughing again. I never imagined being with him could be this easy. He has this way of getting past my defenses.

An hour later, we are sitting at his dining table, pizza box open between us, laughing about how the night has gone. He pours me another glass of wine. The candlelight flickers on the table, giving the moment a kind of intimate warmth that surprises me.

"So," I say, taking a sip of wine and setting the glass down. "What's next on the list of grand romantic gestures?"

He facepalms his forehead. "Shit."

I immediately tense. "What?"

"I forgot the fucking flowers."

Immediately, I reassure him. "I don't need flowers."

He leaps to his feet. "They're in the fridge. Just stay right there."

I close my eyes in anticipation. Even as I hear him rustling around in his fridge, I think of the discussions interspersed with comfortable silence, the kind of silence where I didn't feel the need to fill it with words. This whole evening has been perfect. Just being here with him, sharing pizza and wine in a way that felt surprisingly... normal.

In a way maybe this won't let me down the way my father did.

I frown. *Now, where did that thought come from?*

"Sorry. It took me a minute to move...B? Is everything okay?" Parker's voice is anxious.

My eyes pop open. That's when I see the "flowers" Parker bought for me. Right before I burst into gales of laughter.

In Parker's arms are twelve long-stemmed chocolate roses.

Sheepishly, he admits, "I tried to order roses though Peapod, but they substituted these. I was so worried about the food I forgot to change the flowers to something real."

I lean forward and pull his face toward mine. I'm still grinning as our lips touch in a kiss. It's a good thing the flowers are chocolate because the most romantic part of the evening is when he drops all twelve Dove chocolate roses to sweep me out of the chair as he strides down the hall toward his bedroom.

In the PAST

Bethany

In the shadows of his bedroom, Parker deposits me by the side of his bed. There's no time for nerves because one hand cups the side of my neck, pulling me up so his lips cover mine.

This isn't a tentative kiss. This isn't gentle. This is a show of dominant hunger. Even as he takes from my lips, I find myself giving more and more. Each connection of our lips drives the lust and hunger between us skyrocketing higher.

His other hand cups my hip before slowly making his way upward beneath my top, resting just beneath my rib cage. In answer to his unasked question, I move my arms from where they've been holding on to him like a life raft and lift them. Then *swoosh*, my top is pulled up and over my head.

I'm not quite certain where he's flung it, nor do I care because between one inhale and the next, his hand is cupping my lace-covered breast—calloused fingers twisting and pinching my pebbled nipple. I moan into the base of his neck.

We've shared kisses, hell, we've made out over the months of dating, but until tonight, I've never thrown caution to the wind and just wanted. Just absorbed without restraint. Accepted there would be no turning back from what Parker makes me feel.

He lifts his head and in his silver eyes, recognition of what I'm agreeing to flares.

By the end of tonight, Parker and I will be one.

Our next kiss rockets through me, his tongue stroking in and out of my mouth. He's daring me to chase after him the same way I've kept him on his toes since the day we reconnected. I accept the challenge, nipping his lower lip.

One of his hands slips away from my breast and I release a frustrated moan. That is until his hand slides down my back, into the gap of my jeans, and clasps my bare ass.

Sensations flood my system—heat from where his skin meets mine, chills where the air touches my bareness. I want Parker to speed up even as I need him to slow down. I want to feel this way forever.

Frantically, I arch back and catch sight of the expression on Parker's face. His high cheekbones are flagged with a deep red, his lips are swollen from where I took the nip. Suddenly, I'm as frantic to get to his broad chest as he was to get to mine. Reaching up, I go for his collar. Holding his eyes, I grip the neck and pull with all my might.

Buttons fly in every direction. In my haze of lust, I hear one ping off glass. His breathing accelerates, even as he shrugs out of the mess of what's left of his shirt. The second the cuffs clear his thick wrists, he lets the remains fall to the floor before yanking me back into his arms. Parker's lips crash back down on mine.

Christ, how is it possible for a man to emit such body heat? I wonder as my fingers skim the plane of his chest. My knees go bone-less even as he swoops me off my feet to deposit me on the island of a bed in the center of his room. My pussy clenches in time with my womb contracting as he attacks my clothing—doing his level best to shred my construction boots and socks with his bare hands. If it wasn't for the passion overtaking us both, I have little doubt he could render the material of both useless. Instead, he snaps the laces before bitching, "What the fuck did you do, double knot them?"

"Yes," I manage, shocked.

He snarls, "Next time, don't." Then he slaps at my hands, which are frantically trying to unbutton his dress slacks. "You first."

I bare my teeth. "Get them off or find them in the same condition."

He leans his head down and buries it in the crook of my neck. His lips trail up and down the side even as he flicks open the front clasp of my bra. Now, my unbound breasts have the friction they've been yearning for as he moves his large and impossibly hard body against mine. I arch up against him even as he begins to pull back. Dragging a hand down the center of my body, Parker quickly relieves me of my jeans, leaving me clad in only a thong. "Christ, you're beautiful. I've thought so since the moment we first met."

He levers himself back on top of me. I immediately wrap my legs around his trim waist and my arms around his impossibly broad shoulders. "Parker...please." I'm not above begging for the pleasure I know this man can give to me. Before, the tiny nibbles had been accomplished with him sucking on my breasts, his fingers inside me. Or my hand down his pants, wrapped around what I know is his sizable cock.

Tonight, I want all the pieces put together.

After another earth-scorching kiss, he slides his body down mine. His lips and fingers trace every inch of skin available to him along the way. I moan as they brush over the tops and sides of my breasts, even as his lips capture my nipples in long draws. After he releases them, he drags his fingers along each of my ribs while his body follows the natural line of my stomach—past my belly button to the swollen folds that hide my throbbing clit. His fingers skim over the smooth outer plane before he parts the small strip of hair. Lifting my knees onto his shoulders, he hums his appreciation. "Slick and wet for me, B. That's the way I want you every damn night you're in my bed."

His calloused thumbs peel my petals back right before he drops his head and sucks me into his mouth. My feet plant against his broad back as I rock my hips against his mouth, the pleasure so extreme I'm afraid I might scream down his condo.

The way Parker eats me out is a perfect mirror to the way he lives his life—focused, determined, and superior. Not long after he began focusing on my clit, my world exploded. The moan that escaped me after my release was long and worshiping.

As it should be.

But Parker wasn't done. He fluttered his tongue deep inside me, whether to taste as much of me as he could or to leave an everlasting imprint of himself on me. I'm not certain. Either way, over and over, he brings me back to the precipice.

Then, abruptly, he stands—ripping my thong off my body right before he sheds his pants and reaches for the nightstand drawer to grab a condom.

In the few seconds where I am not in a haze of all things Parker, I take in his naked body while he strokes the condom down his cock. I knew he is big, thick. But even having pumped his cock until it sprayed in my hand one night while making out on his couch, I'm not even certain I am prepared for the sheer beauty of it, the perfection of him.

Yes, his body bears the scars he acquired from the dedication of it to his country, but even in its marked imperfection of scars and burns, never had God ever made a more perfect man. I squirm around the bed as he climbs back on it.

As he crawls between my spread thighs, he pauses, "Are you

certain, B? If you're not ready, I can wait. It's enough that I pleasured you."

It's at that moment I realize I love him. This big, overbearing, autocratic man. We're on fire for each other, and here he is willing to give me more time. Instead of pushing him away, I pull him closer. "Come into me, Parker."

There is no way I could prepare for the way my heart flutters at the idea of how "us" would feel when he pushes in slowly, doing his level best not to hurt me. His cock wedges itself inside me, stretching me, causing my sensitive nerves to once again dance—only this time they ripple along his cock. He groans as he finally seats himself, "Dreamt about this."

I slide my fingers into his hair and yank. He jerks his head back so his eyes meet mine. My voice is a rasp when I whisper, "Same. Now, make my dreams come true."

"With pleasure." With that final permission, Parker takes possession of my body. His hips withdraw his cock before snapping forward with a powerful thrust. Over and over, he plunges his hips, determined to elicit the most powerful pleasure my body's ever known.

I'm no passive player. My hands are in his hair, on his face. Nails clawing down his back, hips. Our lips are never more than scant inches apart. When he drives inside me the final time, I can't hold what's in my heart back. Flinging my head forward, I whisper, "I love you," into his ear as I come on his cock.

I'm not certain he's heard me.

Parker keeps thrusting, his grunts coming faster and faster until he tenses. My name is a shout off the walls when his cock finally explodes with his release—the latex catching the explosion. After, he collapses heavily on me before shifting to the side.

Long moments later, as I drag my hands up and down his back, he murmurs, "Don't think I didn't hear you."

I just reply with a non-committal, "Hmm." My feelings are my own. It doesn't matter if they're never reciprocated, I'm not afraid. I know a part of me will always live on with this man, just as I'll always carry a part of him with me.

He braces himself over me. Brushing my damp hair off my face, he stares down into my eyes. "I will always regret walking away—"

"You mean running," I correct him with a grin because it no longer matters. I know why he left me in Mexico, though I still like to give him grief over it.

His lips brush mine. "I still regret it because if I hadn't, maybe there would have been a chance I could have introduced my parents to the woman I love before they died."

My hands push his hair off his forehead. "I know you wish they were—" *Did he just say what I think he said?* My heart begins a rapid staccato in my chest.

He smirks. God, that smile. It makes me want to love him and choke him at the same time. Then I think, *Why can't I do both?*

With that in mind, I use every ounce of strength I possess to roll Parker. With his bulk, he must let me. There's no other way I'd be straddling him. My hands rest on his heart, my hair falling forward to make a curtain between us. "Care to repeat that?"

He curls up so he can wrap me in his arms. "How about I just say it?"

"Why don't you?"

He rubs his thumb along my cheekbone before he brushes his lips against mine. His expression is softer than any time I've ever seen it. His lips touch mine as he whispers, "I love you, Bethany McCallister. That's no lie. That's a promise I'll keep forever."

"I sure hope so because you're stuck with me," I warn him.

He barks out a laugh before rolling me back on the bed.

18

Present QUESTIONS

PARKER

"Have you ever been involved in any form of fraud or deception?"

I roll my eyes. "This is the stupidest question."

"Why's that?"

"We work for the Agency. We *all* have been involved in deception. It's practically part of our job description."

Fox opens her mouth, but Pamola pipes in, "He's got you there."

She snaps, "My job doesn't involve deception."

I drawl, "Really, Fox? Do you go home and tell your non-cleared spouse, partner, family member what you actually do for a living? Who you work for?" Before she can answer, I point a wired finger in her direction. "Because if you do, not only are you fired and this interview is over, but you've been lying to your co-workers. Thus, deception. And if you haven't, you're just as deceptive as anyone else."

She crosses her arms. "Then what did *you* say to your wife?"

I smirked. "Bethany was cleared."

"Not to the levels she is today."

My smile fades. "No. You're right. And there were times when trust was harder, but Bethany's always known I've worked for the Agency."

Fox leans against the wall. "What times were tough?"

Immediately my mind conjures up the troubled patch our relationship hit when it came to the forefront that someone was following me.

And Libby.

Right before I offered Bethany my life, heart, and soul on a platter to do with what she wished.

In the PAST

Bethany

I slam my hand down to disconnect the call and say to the room at large, "Why do men believe throwing their sweaty, hairy balls on the table means shit? Does this date back to someone pandering to their egos about Homo erectus?"

The entirely female design team sitting around my conference table snickers with laughter before offering up different opinions about the blatantly sexist meeting we just navigated our way through while I seethe inside. Somehow, some way, I managed to not pick up my sledgehammer and remodel the nuts of the pricks that just walked out the door claiming they were doing us a favor by hiring us. While it isn't the first time this has happened in my career, it rubs me raw this time.

I blame Parker.

Maybe that's because today's our one-year anniversary, and I had some major plans to share with my boyfriend—all of which the United States government blew out of the water with their last-minute demand that he fly to Boston to meet with a potential recruit.

Why today of all days? I bemoan silently. Having Parker Thornton as a boyfriend is a challenge on any good day that ends in a Y. Even as I've been keeping secrets from him, well, I'm just impressed his massive cock hasn't tried to fuck the truth from me. *Then again,* the voice inside me reminds me. *It's different.* He has no way of guessing what happened.

I twiddle with my mother's wedding ring, twisting it on the chain around my neck. No one knows. Not even my closest friends, including Libby. Her southern drawl is exaggerated when she offers her opinion, "Because, bless their hearts, they're the sons of the men Linc did business with, B."

My face twists with a smirk. "Ahh, Libs. So tactful."

"I try to be."

"I don't have time for it. I'm dating Thorn."

"Hmm, true." Considering Libby has known my boyfriend longer than I have, she knows what a stubborn pain in the ass he can be. Instead of taking offense to her next comment, I nod sagely when she remarks, "You must need a two-by-four to get your point across with that man."

"I've generally found withholding sex to work better." Something must show on my face because Libby buries her head in her hands, saying, "I don't want to know."

I redirect the conversation. "So, what should we do?"

"About your man?" Libby jokes, causing me to subtly bristle.

It would be too much to hope Libby didn't notice.

Eyes boring into mine, she reaches across the table for a copy of our neatly printed proposal. The project stood to earn McCallister Construction about ten million dollars in profit if we'd stayed on schedule. Deja Vu would have earned double that. As cool as she can be, Libby tears the proposal in half.

My jaw hits the floor, as do the rest of the members of the deal team who spent countless hours working on the bids. I shout, "Are you out of your mind, Libs?"

She angles her chin downward until her eyes bore into mine. "No. In fact, *I'm* feeling rather sane." Her emphasis on the word goes unnoticed by everyone except for me.

Heart pounding, I admit to myself this showdown has been a long time coming, and what better day for it than a day Parker's flying away from where I am. Maybe I'll be able to get some answers from the woman who helped save my father's life, befriended me, and re-introduced me to my boyfriend before...I shake my head to will away the thoughts of the package delivered to this office just a few days ago. Instead, I announce, "Libby and I need the room, please. Everyone leave your copy of the final bid on the table in front of you."

Quickly, but what feels like eons to me, everyone exits the room, leaving Libby and me alone—each of us on one side of the conference table. "Bethany, what's wrong?"

Is there an easy way to ask this? Deciding there's no way to do this other than to just blurt it out, I stare into her green eyes and demand, "Are you fucking Parker?"

Her jaw falls open before her green eyes kindle into dangerous flames. "We're friends. You and me. My husband and Thorn. How dare you ask me something as insulting—"

Interrupting her, I slide the file folder with the pictures that were delivered to my office about ten days ago. Incriminating photos. Pictures of him and Libby going into restaurants. Nose-to-nose. Heading into elevators. Walking into hotel lobbies. Into rooms where my boyfriend has held the door open for her. Very incriminating from the outsider's point of view.

All of this has occurred over the last month. A month where my boyfriend's been distracted with "work" and has only made love to me a few times. A month where he's been late and unavailable for our usual lunches.

Because he's been with her.

Libby's face pales. "Oh. My. God."

I lift my booted feet up and cross them at the ankle atop the now destroyed bid. A bid I went after despite wanting nothing to do with this potential home-wrecker who claimed over and over to care for me, for my family, ever since the death of my mother. Because it would be good for business. I'm grateful it's been killed since I want nothing more than to be as far away from this woman as possible.

As Libby flips through the photos, her hands tremble. The guilt oozing from her pores gives my bruised and battered heart the answer it needs. But it isn't until Libby lifts her face to meet mine and I spy the absolute fury on hers that I realize I may have got it wrong.

Completely wrong.

Her voice is tight when she admits, "I've been helping Thorn plan something special for the two of you—for tonight."

My legs, nothing more than weak noodles, slide off the table and, due to my boots, land with a loud thud. "Excuse me?"

Everything I've imagined since I received those photos shifts as the details move to make room in my mind for a different explanation. "Thorn isn't cheating on me?"

Libby reaches across the table and takes my hand. "He's trying to plan the surprise of a lifetime from the most unromantic guy who walks this earth. We're all in on it, Bethany—everyone from Deja Vu, most of your staff, Cal, our kids."

Tears drip from my eyes. "I'm so sorry, Libs. It just hurt so much to think..."

"Bethany, why didn't you just confront Parker?"

"Because he's been dodging me."

"That's no reason not to demand an answer."

I explain how much Parker has pulled back from intimacy—both physically and emotionally. "And you know how good he is at avoidance."

Libby stares at me intently for a long while. "I think you're going to be very surprised at how much he does think about you."

I twist my fingers together anxiously. "I love him, Libs."

"I know you do."

20

Present QUESTIONS

PARKER

I internally groan. I've already shared so much about my past with Bethany. So much more than I have in any other poly. I try to obfuscate with, "I asked. She answered. We've been married for ten years."

Fox's eyes bore into mine. "You are not a romantic, sir."

Yes, I am. For one woman and one woman only.

I glare at her and try again. "How are these details in any way pertinent to my clearance?"

A cat-like smile crosses her face. "Sir, you know as well as I do it all comes down to the details when we investigate personnel at your level."

Fuck. Why did I have to train so many agents so well? I mentally curse myself for being a fool to think she wouldn't go down this avenue. My head moves slightly to the right, where I look through the two-way glass. Notwithstanding everything that happened yesterday, I can feel her presence somewhere nearby.

Loving me the way no one else can or ever will.

21

TEN YEARS AGO—AGE 34

In the PAST

PARKER

For the last two months, I've been planning to propose to Bethany with a trip back to Texas first so I could do so with the people she loves the most as well as give me the opportunity to tell her father I plan on marrying his daughter.

I don't plan on asking anyone but my B for anything.

I enlisted Libby's help because despite Bethany being his daughter, Libby may know Linc McCallister's state of mind better than any other person on the planet. After all, they were the reason the other survived a kidnap and rescue aboard a cruise they had each taken over a decade ago. A cruise Bethany's mother never came home from.

I know Bethany wears her mother's wedding band around her neck like a talisman, so I wasn't sure if her father was planning on giving the man she loved the corresponding ring. Should I pick out an engagement ring to compliment it or find an entirely new set? I decided on a set she could wear all the time with her work in construction. If she wants her mother's ring reset, we could make it into a pendant.

Libby has been happy to act as the go-between and is thrilled for both Bethany and me. Now, she's calling me to let me know someone has been taking incriminating photos of the two of us. Sniffling, she tells me, "I've let Cal know, Thorn. He's already analyzed them."

My jaw clenches, and I growl into the phone, "Why didn't you come to me first?"

"Because I went to Cal."

Then why didn't Bethany come to me? I wonder as I storm out of the jeweler with Bethany's rings the same afternoon I've touched down from my trip to MIT, where I've recruited a savant hacker into doing contract work for the Agency.

"You haven't been here. Remember?"

"Remember? How can I forget? This trip was three times as long as I expected." God, I'm going to have my hands full with this new recruit to the Agency. A mild admiration fills me. Leanne Miles is no pushover. She'll be a great addition—after I teach her who the fucking boss of this team is. Focusing back on Libby and the photos, I demand coldly, "What does he have to say?"

"He said to call him."

After a quick goodbye, I dial Cal. His first words are, "Go buy a burner and call me back."

Fuck. This isn't going to be good. I stop at the closest store that sells them, pay with cash, and immediately ring him back. As soon as he picks up and verifies it's me, he asks, "Why does your current boss have a hard-on for you?"

I've barely taken two steps down M Street and almost run into a tourist. She started reaming me out. My weak "Excuse me?" was both to her and Cal.

She flings her hand up at me, but he keeps going. "Yeah. He's monitoring your every movement outside the office, Thorn. I sicced

Sam"—Sam Akin is Cal's cousin-in-law and one of the world's fore-most hackers—"on it. He's got you tagged with some kind of tech that would be undetectable. Fortunately, Sam's better or more diabolical, depending on how you look at it, than the people you have working in your labs."

"How long?" I grit out.

"At least the last six months. Sam can't trace back before that."

"Where?"

Cal pauses, asking, "Do you really want me to answer that?"

A hot ball of fire burns inside my chest. I duck down an alley before I hiss, "Yes, it fucking matters, Sullivan. Because if he was watching B, then..."

There's nothing more agonizing than the sound of silence when all you want are words to make your pain dissipate. Flatly, I state, "I'm going to kill him."

It will cost me nothing. Not a single night's sleep. I've murdered people. I've killed on order, taken lives without shame. But this? Bringing my Bethany in as a pawn to a game she only partially under-stands—one she can only be fully briefed on once she marries me—I will take great pleasure in this.

"Thorn," Cal starts.

"Can we hurry this up? I've got places to go and someone to kill," I spit out.

"You can't kill him."

"Why the fuck not?"

He releases a beleaguered sigh before admitting, "They're testing you."

"What the fuck do you mean, Sullivan?"

"They're doing this as part of your clearance reinvestigation."

"Excuse me?" I shout.

"Now, Thorn," he tries to placate me.

"How the fuck do you know this?"

"Sam tripped a wire," he admits.

"Sam tripped the wire on purpose," I fume.

"You're right. But, Thorn, you're in a position they need to know how she'll react. You and I know this won't be the last time she'll be presented with evidence like this if she stays with you and you continue to be—"

"Fuck that. My own fucking agency sent her pictures implying I was with your woman?" Cal sucks in a deep breath. *Yeah, unable to swallow the agony of that quite down. Can you, buddy?* "They dared to threaten my relationship with the only woman I'll ever love. They caused her pain. Now it's my turn to cause some in equal measure."

"Thorn," Cal's warning just starts when the phone is lifted from my ear. I whirl around and find myself face-to-face with my boss. I don't give two shits that I might be unemployed after this.

I throw a fist, relishing in the fact it connects with his jaw. He stumbles back, hand lifting to the red swollen spot.

I couldn't care less the agents that follow him immediately draw their weapons on me. Instead I get right in Director McConaghie's face and bellow, "Are you trying to ruin my relationship before I have the chance to propose to her?"

He has the good grace to look ashamed. Then he says, "We're in the middle of a public street. Let's take this back to the office."

But I stand my ground in defiance of the weapons trained on me. I openly declare warfare between me and my boss. "I won't be going back to my office if these are the kind of back alley scare tactics you'll be using against my future wife to test her loyalty. You'd better think twice. No, you know what? Take this as my formal resignation and shove this job up your fucking ass." Then because it was trained into me from the time I was a young boy, I tack on, "Sir."

The agents holding me hostage in the alley waiver in the absolute confidence in my voice. Their weapons begin to lower even as their eyes cut over to see the director's next response.

He holds his hands out placatingly. "Thorn, there's no need—"

I yell, interrupting him. "There's every need! Has she ever shown any disloyalty to her country?"

"No."

"Ever fell prey to a honey trap?"

"No, Thorn. You're right."

"Have I? Have I ever fucked some hostile agent? Releasing our national security secrets in pillow talk?"

The agents' heads are flipping back and forth between us faster than a tennis volley between Maria Sharapova and Serena Williams.

"No. Thorn, you're right. It's just—"

"It's everything!" I jab a finger in his direction and sneer. "You will call Bethany in and explain what happened."

He sputters. "I'll do no such thing."

"Then my resignation stands." I move to shove by him, noting the admiration I'm garnering from his team. Whether it's because I'm refusing to stand for his underhanded bullshit or because of the fact I'm protecting my woman, I couldn't care less. The fact is, I'm not playing.

Everything to do in my life with Bethany will come first. Now. Always.

Forever.

I've reached the mouth of the alley when McConaghie shouts, "Fine! Bring her by the office. I'll explain."

Shifting my jaw back and forth, I only pray she'll forgive me enough to listen to the bastard. There's only one way to find out.

22

Present QUESTIONS

PARKER

Fox is enthralled. "Did he? Did former Director McConaghie apologize?"

I nod curtly even as I verbalize my response. "Yes."

"To your wife?"

"Yes."

"What did she do?"

A satisfied smirk crosses my face. "She didn't say a single word."

Fox's eyes gleam, but she manages to restrain her amusement. "What did that make you feel?"

I don't even hesitate. "Proud. Bethany is the strongest woman I know."

"Did it make you love her more?"

"No."

Fox is surprised. "No?"

"Nothing could make me love her more when she was, is, and always will be everything to me." With a crooked smile, I say something to Fox, causing her jaw to fall to the floor—and giving myself a reprieve from questions for just a moment. "And that's what I said to her when I proposed."

In the PAST

Bethany

The sky above my father's land is rich with shades of pink and orange as the sun dips low over fields of flowers whose heads seem to droop in the setting sun. I point out to Parker as we stand on the edge of the field, "They're like little soldiers taking a power nap before the sun comes back up to order them to work."

He buries his head in the crook of my neck, lips smiling against the skin bared there.

Right now, this trip home is the perfect distance we needed between what I found out this week about the photos. I'm still in shock over who sent them—the freaking director of the Agency, for Pete's sake! More importantly, *why* they'd been set.

It was a test. I still don't know if I passed or failed. Parker has reassured me he doesn't give a fuck. In fact, I grin as I tip my head back and let the late summer heat still lingering wash over me, he told me so in those exact words before we boarded a plane to fly home. "I already threatened to resign if he didn't own up to what he did."

My jaw unhinged. "What would you do?"

He shrugged as if walking away from all his service in government wasn't a big deal. Still devilment danced in his eyes when he replied, "I thought I'd hit Cal up for a job."

I clasped his shoulders as I straddled his lap and said seriously, "It'd be the end of the world as we know it."

Parker laughed before flipping me down onto the couch and loving me breathless.

Now, we're wrapped up in each other and the kind of Texas evening that reminds me of why I love my home—where the smells of sweet flowers, earth, and the faint scent of barbecue make everything feel grounded and familiar. The only missing piece after all these years is still my mother. Reaching between us, I finger the chain with her ring around my neck and let out a longing sigh.

What would she think about the man I brought home to meet the family? I wonder.

Ellie, Abe, and Jordan are starstruck by him. Jordan has been peppering him all night about his SEAL training. Parker has answered each and every question seriously, not dismissing my sibling in any way. What he did warn him with a quick glance at my father was, "It will change you fundamentally in ways you need to be prepared for."

But my greatest shock was when Thorn and my dad didn't wait for me to introduce them before they were greeting one another, emotions thick in the air. I'd never put it together before then that Parker was part of the SEAL team that rescued my father from the hell he endured when he and my mother were kidnapped on their anniversary cruise.

When my father asked me how I could not know, I shot a furious look at my boyfriend. His response made my heart melt. "I wanted Bethany to fall in love with me, Linc. I didn't want her to fall for a guy who happened to be in a place to carry her dad off a ship when he'd survived hell on his own."

My father snickered. "Modest, as always, Thorn?"

"One of my best features, Linc."

Then, to my and my siblings' shock, the two of them clasped fore-arms and slapped each other on the back. Thorn murmured some-thing in my father's ear, causing his eyes to well up. "Okay, son."

"Son? Did we just adopt Parker?" I nudged into their moment to take my father's temperature, so used to doing it after the first five years after my mother died. I need to make certain he's fine.

Parker reached for my hand and pulled me into their circle before crooning into my ear. "Oh, B. If only the rest of your life was going to be that easy."

His words caused my heart to pound even as I laughed at the amusement dashing away the shadows from my father's eyes.

Now, I lean back against his broad chest and peek upward at Parker, who admires the vast beauty the Texas sun is kissing as it goes to sleep. There is something profound about seeing him here that makes it feel like he has always belonged. He's still danger disguised in dark blue jeans and a fitted shirt that barely stretches across his broad chest, but there is a softness to his expression. After all this time together, I should be used to seeing it, but each time I do, it zings my heart. It's as if all the barriers he keeps up against the world have dropped and he can freely demonstrate his love without reservations.

Tonight feels different though. Regardless of the surety and protection I feel within his arms, there is a tension in the air, some-thing unspoken between us that has been building. Ever since he spoke to my father, I can feel it. No, that's a lie. I've felt it every time he's looked at me since he came back from his recruiting trip to MIT, and he uncovered the source of who sent me those photos. It's more profound, almost tangible. Something that makes my heart beat just a little faster every time our eyes connect.

"You're quiet," I say, squeezing the arm wrapped around me. "What has you thinking so hard?"

He smiles down at me, a soft chuckle escaping his lips. "Do you think your father will recover from the fact we're together?"

Flippantly, I reply, "Oh, he won't. You've officially made it so Ellie can never bring a man home."

Parker's silver eyes catch the last bit of sunlight. There is a seriousness in his expression now, and it makes me pause. "I think he likes me though," he says, his voice quieter, more thoughtful.

"He does. More importantly, he respects you. Trust me, if he didn't, you'd know by now. One thing my dad doesn't do is hide his feelings." Lord knows he didn't for the longest time.

Parker smiles again, but it doesn't quite reach his eyes this time. He seems... nervous. I tilt my head to the side, trying to get as much of his face in my view as I can. "What's going on with you tonight? You're acting weird."

"I've just been thinking."

"About?"

"About you. About us. About... the future."

I blink, not sure what to say. I didn't expect that, not tonight. Not here, of all places. "Parker, does this have anything to do with what your boss tried to do? I'm sorry. I should have come to you."

He spins me in his arms and lays a finger over my lips. "We talked about that. You did what you felt you needed to do. You confronted Libby because she was there. You were going to confront me when I got back, but then I dragged you to my boss's office."

I nod. It played out exactly like that, with Cal and Libby's fury equal to my own. Parker's boss didn't earn himself any favorability that day. In fact, rumors are swirling on television that there may be a new director in the near future. I wonder if that might be the man in front of me. "Then what are you—"

But before I can finish, he lifts my left hand, his thumb brushing over my knuckles. His touch grounds me as a wave of realization hits me. With the twilight illuminating the sky, the same time of night he ran away from our first kiss, with that same intense gaze he had that first night—the one that made me feel like I was the only person in the world who mattered—he lifts my hand to his mouth and kisses it. "I love you, B," he says, his voice steady but reverent. "I knew you were different from that first day in Mexico, but I think I started falling the night we reconnected in Cal and Libby's living room and you ignored me."

My heart knocks against my ribs. "I didn't—"

"You absolutely did," he interrupts, grinning. "And I knew right then that I was in trouble. You were everything I didn't know I was missing. I just hate we could have had this sooner."

I swallow hard, the lump in my throat growing as his words penetrate. This isn't just a casual conversation amid the budding moonlight. This might be everything.

Parker cradles my fingers against his cheek, but I can see a slight tremble in his hand. "Do you want to know what I whispered to your father today?" he asks.

"What?" My heart's thundering so hard I wonder if it's going to stop.

His eyes never leave mine. "I told him I was going to marry you."

For a second, the world seems to stop spinning. My breath catches in my chest, and all I can do is stare at him, my mind racing to catch up. Then his words penetrate, and my lips curve. "You didn't ask?"

Parker snorts. "No. He's not the person I love. There's only one person I plan on asking." With that, he twists my hand and presses his lips to the center of my palm.

My body trembles.

"You saw his reaction," Parker continues, a soft smile tugging at his lips. "But, B? None of that means a damn thing without this." He drops to one knee in front of me, pulling a small, simple velvet box from his pocket.

I gasp, my hands flying to cover my mouth as tears well up in my eyes. This is really happening. This man—this strong, successful, arrogant, obnoxious man—is proposing to me. At my family's home. Making new happy memories for me where so much pain lived. Burying the past and building our future on top of it.

"Bethany." He looks up at me with so much love in his eyes that it nearly knocks the breath out of me. "I want to spend the rest of my life with you. I want to laugh with you, and argue with you, and screw up a million more dinners with you. You're everything I never knew I needed. My parents would have loved you and I hope like hell your mother would have tolerated me."

I laugh even amid my tears. I'm already nodding yes, but I can't get the word out.

Parker continues, "You're strong and smart, and with you by my side, I know I can be a better man."

"Who in this world could be better than you?"

His whole body shudders. "Will you marry me?"

Tears spill down my cheeks. My voice catches in my throat. "Yes," I whisper. "Yes, I'll marry you."

A huge grin breaks out across his face as he surges to his feet. Before I can throw myself into his arms, he quickly slips the ring my eyes are too wet to see onto my finger before pulling me into his arms. His heart is racing against mine as he hauls me up on my toes to kiss me with unrestrained passion. For a moment, everything else falls away. The world narrows down to just the two of us—the girl who grew up to play with tools and the boy who grew up to protect the world. Neither of us quite fit in, yet somehow, we're a perfect fit for each other.

When we finally pull apart, I can't help but laugh through my tears. "You snuck in asking my dad right in front of my face?"

Parker chuckles, wiping a tear from my cheek with his thumb. "Well, I didn't want him completely unaware."

Then I'm reminded of the photos. "And Libby?"

His smile is tender. "Look at your ring."

I do and gasp. It's a non-traditional engagement ring—an eternity band. He admits, "I kept bringing Libby to meet with the jewelers because I knew I wanted you to be able to wear your ring, but I didn't know what the hell to buy."

"Oh, Parker." My voice is breathless as my finger runs over the fully faceted diamonds. They'll only get in the way if I accidentally nail my hand with a hammer. Much less likely than having a solitaire. I lift the hand now bearing the symbol of his love to cup his face. "You did perfectly."

A breath of air whooshes out of his lungs. I frown. "She said everyone was involved in something."

"Yeah." At my raised brow, he admits, "They're planning our engagement party for when we get home."

My heart feels so full I think it might burst. "You're so cocky, it's ridiculous."

"And you love me for it," he teases, leaning in for another kiss.

"Yeah," I whisper against his lips, smiling. "I really do."

"B?"

"Yes?"

He lifts my hand to his heart. "I'm over the moon you said yes to marrying me, but the real day I said I do was the day you said you loved me. Nothing could make me love you more when you always will be everything to me."

24

Present QUESTIONS

PARKER

I'm singularly unsurprised when Fox asks, "How long after you proposed to your wife till you were married?"

My eyes roll in her direction. "Did you do *any* research before you came in the door today? I mean, I do have better places to be than strapped here."

"I couldn't tell from your cooperative attitude."

I bang my head on the back of the chair only to be reminded by Deere, "Sir, could you avoid moving? It will cause a problem with your readings."

"Right."

Fox is incredulous. "How come you're not a sanctimonious prick when addressing him?"

"Because he's not asking me ridiculous questions. He's pointing out a technical problem that I'm causing."

"So if I'd asked you a question such as, 'Do you remember who the DJ was for your wedding?' I wouldn't be on the receiving end of your attitude?"

"Correct. For the record, the answer to your question is DJ Kensington."

Deere splutters, Pamola makes a noise, and Fox follows up to confirm, "Do you mean *the* DJ Kensington? Worldwide sensation? Number one artist of 'Curses on the Mend,' that DJ Kensington?"

Cheerfully, I beam, "One and the same. Though she was just Austyn back then. A precocious fourteen."

Fox is wheezing. She can't even ask her next question, giving me a moment to ask Pamola, "Can I have some water while Fox stops fangirling?"

"Yes, sir." But his own face is starstruck at the idea Bethany and I had the now infamous artist as our wedding DJ long before she was a household name.

25

TEN YEARS AGO—AGE 25

In the PAST

Bethany

Even as I stand on the edge of the dance floor, our vows and rings having been exchanged earlier, I still can't believe it. Parker and I are married.

Friends from all over the world flew in to join our celebration—people I haven't seen in years, friends from college, colleagues from McCallister. I smirk as I spot some of my single girlfriends from Rice mingling with Parker's SEAL buddies—some in dress uniforms, some in sharp suits. All looking good but none looking as fine as the man who stood in front of me not long ago promising me his heart, his soul, and his devotion from now until death do us part.

Still, it makes my heart swell to see everyone together.

People are laughing, dancing, and letting loose—just the way Parker and I wanted. No stiff, formal reception for us. This is a celebration of life and love. I can't think of a better way to cap off the night.

"Austyn Kensington, y'all!" my best friend Lily announces with her hands cupped around her mouth as she bounces by, hyping her up like the proud Texan she is. "This girl is gonna be famous! Just you wait!"

She isn't wrong. Austyn Kensington is a local high school freshman with a serious talent for both musical instruments and mixing tracks. When Parker and I first heard about her through her music teacher at Kensington High, we were looking for a harp player for our wedding ceremony. He not only recommended her to play for the ceremony but also advised us, "If you happen to be looking for a DJ, you couldn't find one better than Austyn."

"Really?" Parker said skeptically.

"Truly. Come listen." Then he led us to the music room where Austyn had been practicing her harp. At his request, she switched over to spinning up some tunes. By the end of her impromptu audition, we were begging him to get in contact with her mother to sign her for our contract. We both knew we had to book her for our wedding. Austyn's energy is contagious. She has this incredible way of reading the crowd that most seasoned DJs would envy.

Now, here she is, a fourteen-year-old spinning tracks that has everyone—from my construction crew to Parker's brothers-in-arms—up and dancing. I've never seen so many men willing to throw down on a dance floor. Austyn whoops it up at the sight of Parker's BUD/S buddy, Kyle, trying to teach her mother how to salsa properly. The very prim and proper Dr. Paige Kensington, who was invited to chaperone her daughter as she lit the night with music, put him in his place. He took his schooling, but the grin on his face said he didn't care.

Parker holds me close as we sway to our first dance, the soft sound of Austyn's harp rendition of Chris Stapleton's "Fire Away" wrapping around us like a warm blanket. His hand firm at the small of my back, his other gently holding mine. He leans in, lips brushing against my temple.

"Happy?" he murmurs, his breath warm against my skin.

"More than I thought possible." Feeling the peace settle deep in my chest. "You?"

"More than I ever believed I could be," he says, his voice low, throbbing. "This is just our beginning."

"What's been your biggest surprise so far?"

"How stunning you were coming down the aisle to me. Jesus, B. I almost had a heart attack."

I raise an eyebrow at him. "Oh? I thought for sure the biggest surprise was hiring a fourteen-year-old DJ."

Parker chuckles, the sound vibrating through his chest, and I can't help but snuggle closer to feel it vibrate against my body. "Next to marrying you, hiring Austyn's the best decision we made."

I agreed, and we continued to dance for hours before mingling together and separately. But even as the excitement continues to buzz around me, I feel a pang deep in my chest when I spy my father on the fringes of the crowd talking with Libby and Cal. My mother should've been here. She should've been in the room with me, helping me dress, adjusting my veil, dabbing the tears of joy from my cheeks when I received Parker's letter before the ceremony. Instead, while I'm grateful for Libby's and my sister's presence, there is an emptiness that couldn't be filled. In all the time since she's been gone, I've never felt her absence more than I did today.

Taking a deep breath, I shake off the sadness. Today is about joy, about love—about the life Parker and I have committed to building together. Mama would've wanted me to focus on that.

Before I can move, I feel a strong arm slip around me. His lips graze my neck. "Happy, B?"

"Very. You?"

"You're my wife. That's all I need." Leaning back against him, I let him absorb my weight as we take in the family we've made. I know he, too, is missing the presence of his parents today. We honored them during the ceremony by lighting a candle for each of them in floating water before we spoke our vows. He looked so handsome in his tux, his usually sharp and intense features softening when he caught sight of my father escorting me down the aisle. He didn't look like the man willing and able to order people into countless dangers or who'd faced enemies himself. Parker just looked like a man who would move heaven and earth to love me forever.

The music begins to play softly, the signal that it is time for me to throw the bouquet before our last dance. We make our way to the center of the dance floor, me holding my bouquet—a mix of sunflowers, irises, and roses. Even as I take my place, I only have eyes for Parker. Standing at the end of the dance floor, his gaze locks on mine, and the moment our eyes meet, my heart trembles with possibilities.

This was right.

Our love is everything.

I feel tears prick from the overwhelming joy of knowing that this man—this brave, strong, stubborn man—is mine. And I am his.

Even as the DJ calls everyone forward, I recall his vows—short, sweet, and simple. The minister spoke of love and loyalty, of standing by one another through thick and thin. But all I could focus on was Parker's hand in mine, the way his thumb brushed against my skin.

When it was time for our vows, Parker cleared his throat, looking down at me with those piercing eyes that had always made me feel like he saw right through to my soul. His voice was deep and a little raspy, "Bethany, I always knew I was lucky as well as blessed. Not because of what I've done, or what I've survived, but because all the roads I took led me to stand here today. At the end, I'd crawl through a desert, fly through any skies, and swim through any troubled waters to be able to call you my wife. I promise you, from this day forward, I'll always be by your side. Whatever comes our way, we'll face it together. Till death do us part."

Tears blurred my vision as I whispered, "I love you."

In the moment under the Texas sky, with my friends and family surrounding us, I knew that no matter what life threw at us—whether it was danger, heartache, or joy—we would face it together.

Holding his heated gaze, I release my bouquet, uncaring who catches it. All I care about is boarding the private plane Parker arranged to take us to Bali to the little hut over the ocean, where I plan on wearing little to no clothing over the next ten days.

Judging by the expression on his face, he's in total agreement with that plan.

26

Present QUESTIONS

PARKER

"Got a problem, Fox?" I taunt.

"Just something in my eye, sir. I just need a moment."

I really want to bust her balls about thinking I wasn't a romantic, but her next question brings me back into focus. "It's been ten years since you and your wife married. No children?"

"No, not yet."

"Do you want them?"

"We both do, eventually."

"Are you waiting for a reason?"

I'm waiting to see if the one she's carrying survived its father shooting its mother last night, I think grimly. "Timing. It all comes down to timing."

And ensuring the threat against my wife doesn't take that dream from us before Bethany even has the chance to tell me.

27
YESTERDAY

In the PAST

PARKER

It's been ten years and my wife can still make my dick harden as rigid as a spike merely by swaying her ass from side to side. Ten years of supporting each other's hopes and dreams. Of going to bed in each other's arms as many nights as we can in spite of two insanely demanding careers.

It's been a decade of knowing that we're more in love today than when we spoke our vows under the Texas sun. All we've done is grow and build the perfect foundation for our future together. I want to spend eternity with her by my side. Maybe with a few mini-B's thrown into the mix. Huh. Maybe tonight I can convince my wife I'm just as ready as she is for a family.

I admire her curves and taut body, loving the throb behind my slacks and pissed as fuck I can't do anything about it despite having originally taken today off. Still, it's a high to know I, and I alone, know that beneath the rough and tumble exterior of a plaid shirt, torn jeans, and worn-in construction boots, few scraps of lace cover her luscious breasts and cup the tantalizing entrance to her pussy.

The first time I saw the entrancing combination in our old condo, I didn't bother to ask my wife why. After all, I'd just fucked her raw during our first time together. Later, after regaining my breath, I recall saying, "Why wear something so uncomfortable?"

She'd just finished picking up the shreds of material I'd torn apart before replying, "Because I *am* a woman, Parker." She smiled mischievously. "And I like shocking my husband."

My wife is one of the few people on the planet who still gets away with calling me by my given name. Hearing it in her lazy Texan drawl never fails to make me want to make her scream it. My eyes roamed her luscious form. "I doubt anyone would deny that, B."

"This is for me—to remind myself of that." Her lips curved even as she concluded, "Though I do enjoy your appreciation of it."

I still do. I did then. I do now, even though she's more than the woman taking my dick on a regular basis. For the last decade, she's been my woman. One I'd die for in a heartbeat.

Just the thought sends chills up my spine as I study her carriage as she makes her way toward the exit of our bedroom. Savagely, I vow the same thing I do every single day. *I will keep her safe, no matter the cost.*

I call out, "Bethany?"

Her head whips around, blond hair settling around her chin. "Yes?"

Dropping the ends of the Silvio Fiorello tie she got me for Christmas about eight weeks ago, I stride to where she's standing and cup her face. "I'm sorry. If there was any other way, I would have rescheduled this."

The disappointment that lit Bethany's eyes when I explained why I might be late for our anniversary party being thrown by the Sullivans at the office of Deja Vu recedes with my apology. She, more than anyone else, knows I have no real control over my schedule. Even being the man in charge, director of an intelligence agency equally feared and revered around the world, there are certain things that I have absolutely no control over.

Today's spectacle is one of them.

She reaches up, her dainty fingers clutching my thick wrists. If it weren't for the callouses on her hands, I'd never have believed this petite beauty could have a strength to match my own. Gorgeous, yes. I knew that already from the first time we met. But the core of steel that makes my wife who she is never ceases to amaze me. Every day I thank a series of gods for bringing Bethany McAllister back into my life. After living a life where I did everything to keep myself from drowning in the abyss, I never imagined I'd have a partner to navigate the troubled waters with me.

I never could have expected her to be strong enough to take on a man like me and all the demons that live inside my soul.

Rising on her toes, as best as she can in her hard-soled shoes, she aims her kiss so her lips will brush against mine gently. I slide my arms around her, intent on fusing our mouths together. I'm begging without words—pleading for forgiveness for something I have absolutely no control over.

Then there's that feeling I can't shake. One that intensified since the phone call to my secure line. Why today?

Why does someone need to interrogate me today about my preliminary clearance paperwork? Shit, that crap isn't due to be re-upped for another six months.

Desperately, I clutch her to me—irrationally fearing if I let go, I'll never see her again. The last time I felt like this, I was a SEAL in hostile territory, and there was a Zodiac I was desperately trying to swim toward with a bullet hole in my shoulder.

Sliding my hands around her, one behind her neck and the other around her waist, I deepen the kiss, telling my wife in no uncertain terms she's who I want to be with today, our wedding anniversary—

not a polygrapher and multiple agents grilling me on any and all aspects of my career.

Again.

Long minutes pass before she pulls back. Her peaches and cream skin is flushed from the intensity of our kiss. Her perfect hair is mussed. Her eyes are several degrees warmer when she pulls back to stare up at me.

This time, I don't feel unsettled when I stare down into my wife's turbulent blue eyes. I'm still frustrated at life for throwing another monkey wrench in our reality. Pressing my forehead against hers, I murmur, "I'll do everything I can."

Her breath comes out in a rush before she relents, "I know you will."

"There's no place I'd rather be than here with you today, B. I love you."

"I love you, Parker." For just a moment, something unguarded filters through my wife's eyes. It flashes through so briefly I can't read it. Her hand reaches up and cups my chin. "You know that, right?"

"Bethany?"

"Later. We'll both be late." She presses her lips against mine one last time before breaking free of my grip.

I want to howl at someone or something for fucking with my plans to woo my wife, to celebrate the two of us, instead hauling my ass into the office. Unfortunately, national security has no patience and doesn't give a shit about sentiment or dates on a calendar.

Still I'm relieved when, at the door to our suite, she turns and says, "Happy anniversary, Parker. Try not to kill anyone."

I grumble, in part to remind her of the torment I'm about to endure. "No promises. You're not the one who will have a rectal probe in their ass."

Her musical laugh remains in my memory long after she leaves the house. Once I'm ready to leave, I press a button on my phone to secure our residence while notifying my security team I'm ready to be driven to my office, just a few minutes' drive from our home in McLean, Virginia.

SITTING in the back of a limousine with more safety features than an armored vehicle, I don't pull out my phone to check one of the hundreds of messages I'm certain are waiting for me. Instead, I abide by the no cell phone use rule I demand all employees of the Agency to abide by as they approach the three-mile mark of our secret entrances off the George Washington Memorial Parkway.

With the way the damn things triangulate off towers, it's bad enough for my heartburn to know the Agency location coordinates are available on Wikipedia. That said, I don't want to encourage employee movement to be tracked within what I consider a safe perimeter. It gives our enemies too much information.

Who travels to work on certain routes.

Who walks in between what buildings for what meetings.

Who works in certain facilities on campus.

All it takes is one small slip up and we'd be dealing with a FUBAR of epic proportions. I've already survived a lifetime of dealing with plans going from fine to fucked up in an instant. And that was before I became the director of one of the most feared intelligence agencies in the world. Now, it's my job to ensure the people who work here are safe and prepared for anything to happen.

Fortunately, I married a woman who understands that—for the most part. Though Bethany does get pissed from time to time, not that I blame her. Take this morning when I got the call that today, on my fucking wedding anniversary of all days, an unexpected polygraph examination was going to be taking place as a result of a mole inside the government with close ties to the President.

I scrub my hand down over my face. When I stood before our family and friends a decade ago, I took vows and meant them.

For better, for worse.

In sickness and in health.

Till death do us part.

I mutter, "Somewhere in there, I don't remember a line item during our ceremony for jobs that believe you're at their beck and call twenty-four hours a day."

One of the assigned agents who guard my every movement outside my home or office pipes up, "Was there something you need, Director Thornton?"

"Nothing." My thoughts turn introspective.

I can't say I blame my wife for being disappointed. While I'm not feeling great about the fact I'm going to be the one who is going to be literally strapped down, have my butt cheeks monitored for pucker action all day long, it's the fact that, once again, I feel like my patriotic duty is causing me to break her heart that has my insides churning.

Grimly, I realize, after everything I had to go through to get Bethany to open her heart, I need her to know I remember that not just today but every day we have together.

28

PARKER

"That was yesterday with"—Fox consults her notes—
"Agents Jarper and Merimanga."

"Yes. They are the ones who called me downstairs."

"At whose orders."

"The orders came through with the presidential code words."

Fox's lips thin, as do Pamola's and Deere's. No one is happy to
have me here today because of my actions last night. Except if I didn't
take my best shot, I wouldn't be sitting here answering questions. I'd
be dead.

As dead as they wanted my wife to be.

"At what point did you realize your wife's life was in danger?"

My fingers clench against the chair. That's when Deere reprimands me, "Director Thornton, please relax. Your heartbeat is accelerating."

I snap, "You try to live through a day like yesterday and not have your goddamn heartbeat accelerate, Deere."

Surprisingly, Fox crouches in front of me. Her eyes met mine head on. "There isn't a single man or woman in this building today who doesn't have your back, sir. And if they don't, they'll be incarcerated. You'll see to it. You know we're here to do a job you trained us to do. We're almost done."

Jaw clenched, I nod. Instead of berating me for not audibly responding, Fox pushes to her feet before offering me a quick drink of water. Then, she repeats her question. "At what point did you realize your wife's life was in danger?"

I get my shit together so I can reply. "When the agents burst in and held the people who were questioning me—like you are right now—at gunpoint."

She swallows. "Right."

"So, if we could wrap this up, I have more important places to be." Like at my wife's hospital bedside.

29
YESTERDAY

In the PAST

PARKER

The outfit I've been ordered to put on after the agents escort me five floors below the Agency's marble logo instead of to my spacious office demands a return of the cold persona I wear every day when I step inside this building. If people thought I was a dick as a SEAL team leader, that doesn't have anything on me as the director of the Agency.

With over twenty thousand people relying upon the decisions I make on a daily basis, I believe wholeheartedly in our unofficial credo. "And ye shall know the truth and the truth shall make you free."

Even as the elevator descends, I recall the events leading up to Bethany leaving our bedroom disappointed this morning. Instead of waking her up by making slow, sweet love, we were both woken by a ringtone we both know all too well—the internal security division. Even I groaned as I flipped the phone open to answer.

"Thornton," I said, my voice gruff with sleep and the warm body next to mine. Bethany, meanwhile, was skimming her hand down over the plane of my stomach, doing her damnedest to distract me.

"Director Thornton, we need you to come in for your polygraph."

My heart stopped for a beat. A polygraph? I hadn't predicted that after I met with the president in the Oval last week. As the head of the Agency, I should've been informed of this ahead of time or at least been given a heads-up. Something. Not an impromptu call while I was ready to sink into my wife on our wedding anniversary

"Authorization codes," I snapped, trying my level best to do my damn job.

"Alpha Bravo Foxtrot. One, Two, Six, Niner. Charlie. Quebec. Eight, Seven. Zulu."

Shit. This week's presidential authorization. Trying to keep my tone neutral, I asked, "What's this about?"

The voice on the other end remained clinical. "Standard protocol, sir. Routine clearance revalidation."

Routine, my ass. Nothing about this call was routine, but I knew better than to push back—at least not until I was sitting in the room.

"Fine," I said. "When do you need me?"

"Now, sir. We're ready for you."

I glanced at the clock. It was barely dawn, and I had plans—plans I'd been looking forward to for weeks. An anniversary party with Bethany. I was looking forward to it, especially the afterparty, after we'd had a little wine and I'd presented her with her favorite roses— the chocolate kind. Now someone—and I knew for certain it wasn't the president—called me in for a damned polygraph.

"Understood," I replied, forcing calm into my voice. "I'll be there shortly."

AN HOUR LATER, I found myself sitting in a windowless room with beige walls and sterile lighting. The polygraph examiner sat across from me, a no-nonsense woman with graying hair pulled into a tight bun. She looks like the kind of person who has no time for small talk—and I respect that.

Except I know for a damn fact she has no right to be questioning someone of my clearance level.

This setup is for someone with a much lower clearance level than I hold.

Everything about this stinks to high heaven. I only hope the coded message I managed to type out on my flip phone from the back of the limo made it through to the Sit Room before I had to shut it off once we reached the Agency radius space.

I adjust myself in the uncomfortable chair. As usual, there are wires from the machine strapped across my chest and arms. I've been through this more times than I can count, but it never gets easier. It isn't the questions themselves—it is what they represent. The constant reminder that in this world, trust was a luxury.

The examiner looks at me over the top of his clipboard. "Ready, Director Thornton?"

"As ready as I'll ever be," I reply, my tone icy.

He starts with the baseline questions, the ones meant to set the tone, to establish my physical responses. "Is your name Parker Thornton?"

"Yes."

"Are you the director of the Agency?"

Geez, didn't I teach these people anything? Lead into the fun questions. Still, I answer, "Yes."

"Are you currently under duress?"

How do you want me to answer this? I'm raging mad over some kind of bullshit happening in my house, but duress? "No."

His voice remains steady as he advances through polygraphy 101 routine questions. It isn't until he attempts to shift toward more sensitive inquiries that the tension in the room starts to shift. "Did you inform the president of a classified data breach involving any US federal government contractors in the past twelve months?"

I pause before answering because the truth is, "No."

He persists, "Are you certain?"

"Yes."

"We've heard you've been taking meetings in the Oval."

I counter, "Who's we?"

I get a snooty counter, "We're the ones asking the questions."

Oh, I'm going to enjoy eating you for lunch when this is done. Trying to divert me, he asks, "Have you been approached by a foreign intelligence service in the past year?"

"No."

"Have you intentionally withheld information from your superiors?"

I pause, just for a fraction of a second, before answering. "No, since I have no superior other than the president."

His eyes flick up, narrowing, but he doesn't comment. We continue like that for what feels like an eternity. Question after question, each one probing deeper into my life, my decisions, my loyalties. I answer them all honestly—of course I do. But still, the process feels like it is circling me around a single-issue drain—the secret investigation the president ordered me to conduct with the head of the Department of Justice about our overseas contractors.

What I want to know is how Tweedle Dee and Tweedle Dumb know about it.

Precious minutes tick away as I endure their fumbling attempt at getting me to trip up. Would it be too obvious if I yawn in their face to get them to speed up? I'm the head of the agency, for fuck's sake. I want to shout at them to come at me and ask me if you have the fucking balls to. Instead, to play the part and not tip my hand, I am strapped to a machine, answering questions about my integrity like the agency head is some kind of cash-for-hire political appointee.

Amid all of this is my worry about Bethany. All my senses are screaming at me at the wrongness of this happening today.

Just when I'm about to leap out of my skin, the door is kicked open. In a split second, I recognize two members of the Presidential Protective Detail, who have guns drawn. Fortunately for my trussed-up ass, they're after Dumb and Dumber fuck. I'm quickly unstrapped as the room is swarmed. "What is the situation?" I demand.

"Sir, the president wants you to contact him on a secure line. Stat."

I bolt from the room. Slapping my palm against a wall, a hidden elevator opens that will take me out of the basement and to the main Agency floor. From there, I don't wait. I sprint past the meandering employees waiting for the lifts to carry them to their floors for the night shift.

I race up the stairs.

Hitting my level, I burst through the doors and race down the corridor to my office. Within moments, I've turned my office into a secured space—I offer up a thanks to my wife for that brilliant feature —and I'm on a video conference with the White House Situation Room. "Sir? What the hell is going on?"

"Thorn, those contractors you were tracking overseas—"

"Yes, sir."

"The DOJ uncovered the link between them this morning."

"And that is?"

"They're all family businesses owned by members of the McConaghie family."

My mind is whirling pulling pieces together. Finally, I croak out, "No."

He's dead.

The look on my face must speak a thousand words because the president admits, "It's his son. He's out for vengeance."

Leaning forward, I order, "I want my wife taken into custody. Right now."

"Thorn, I—"

"What, sir?"

"He's taken the entire top floor of McCallister Construction hostage. Including your wife."

My heart stops beating. *No, it's not possible. I'd know if the other half of my soul was gone.* I'm sure the pressure in my chest is an indicator I'm about to have a heart attack. I know it. Then, certainty flows through me. I'm not going to stand here and wait. I'm going to go and save my wife.

"Sir, I'm going to need immunity."

His face turns cautionary. "For what?"

"To murder the bastards who are holding my wife." Without another word, I disconnect the call and disengage the security so I can leave the office. Even as I race through the building, I'm punching Cal's number since I've missed at least two dozen calls from him and Sam.

"Thorn, where the fuck have you been?" he screams in my ear

"They had me in the basement using a presidential authorization code that checked out," I snarl. "The PPD just rescued me a few minutes ago. Where the fuck am I going?"

Cal's silent for a moment, obviously trying to regain control of his emotions. "What are you planning?"

"After I'm done killing everyone who stops me from getting to my wife?"

"Thorn," Cal begins. Then his next words freeze my forward momentum. My body wants to move, but my legs stop working.

Tears blur my eyes, but I manage to say, "I'll clear you through the gate. Come and get me."

"I'm on my way."

30

Present QUESTIONS

PARKER

"Can you provide details about your last three positions, including job titles and responsibilities?"

My eyes narrow at Fox trying to keep a straight face before I reply with no intonation. "Navy SEAL. Sniper. Associate Director of the Agency. At a high level, I ran several tactical teams. Work, classified. Promoted to director. All current responsibilities classified."

"Sir, with all due respect, we're all cleared in this room."

My lip curls in a sneer. "Do you know what I was doing last night?"

"No, sir."

"Then your clearance damn sure isn't high enough for you to

know what it is I do inside the walls of my office. Now move on to the next fucking question."

Even as Fox opens her mouth to do so, I'm just grateful my heart rate didn't fluctuate because last night's events were definitely not part of the job responsibilities assigned to the director of the Agency. They are, however, the ones I assumed when I tied my life to Bethany's.

To have and to hold.

From this day forth.

Till death do us part.

"I'd like to circle back to a question I asked you this morning."

"Go ahead."

"Why did you kill someone intentionally?"

"Because of my wife, and before you ask, yes. I'd do it again," I immediately answer.

In the PAST

PARKER

I heft the stock of my rifle against my shoulder and glance through the laser sight. I have no shot without taking aim directly through my own heart and soul.

A bead of sweat runs down my temple. Cal was right when he picked me up. "Nothing is going to prepare you for what you're going to see, Thorn. Nothing."

I scoffed. Was I fucking wrong. If I make it out of this without joining my wife in either Heaven or Hell, I'll apologize to Cal for underestimating him. Not my BUD/S training nor the thousands of hours of target practice as I specialized in becoming a SEAL sniper at Camp Pendleton. None of my missions at the Agency, nor any I'd sent my agents on as director, came close to the nightmare I was enduring.

I'd relive the hundreds of hours spent surviving by eating bugs in a swamp and breathing through a reed, all while hiding in plain sight in a ghillie suit just to get her out of the way of the bullet I'll have no choice but to release close to 500 yards away. It's a shot many can make, but I'm one of the few men in this country who can without alerting the perpetrators.

Forcing them to trip the deadman's switch and blow off the top of McCallister Construction.

For all the orders I've coolly followed before it became my time to sit behind the desk and direct my own cadre of agents, I'm being asked to true up my account for each and every decision that ever caused anyone a single ounce of hardship with the convenience of my arrogant pride.

Even though my days are spent behind a desk instead of actively in the field, I'm prepared to do this. I still train as hard as any agent I send into the field, whether that's physically or mentally. Still, I must be getting older. Somehow, this maniac managed to break through multiple layers of defenses I surreptitiously put in place to avoid this very thing as I worked with the president and the DOJ. Somehow my defenses were breached and my heart was stolen right from beneath my nose. They'll pay for that. They'll pay for scaring her.

They'll die if they hurt her.

Shrugging my face against my shoulder to wipe away the imperceptible bead of sweat, I listen through my earbud as other snipers from agencies ranging from state police to other federal agencies make their way to other nearby rooftops. In the briefing we had earlier, I determined the only way to take out this bastard with a minimal number of civilian casualties is if we take all the fuckers out at the exact same time.

What I couldn't factor in was the fact I may as well be signing my own death sentence by doing my damn job.

Till death do us part.

My heart threatens to pound out of my chest when I consider the situation I see inside that office. *If only the person wearing the suicide vest weighed down wasn't her. If I could guarantee she'd react with her head and wouldn't let go of the kill switch in her left hand.* A hand that bears the wedding ring I slipped on not long after we reconnected ten years ago.

Giving myself the briefest of moments, my eyes drift closed. I recall the faint scent of coconut and rum—scents I always associate with her before throwing blind prayers skyward. I don't care if tomorrow I'm waterboarded, hit by a bus, or stabbed in a dark alley. I'll gladly trade in on every heroic thing I've ever done so I don't have to be the one to take the shot.

But God is too busy to listen to a son of a bitch like me if what I just saw through my scope is anything to go by. I need to save a roomful of American lives—my wife and her colleagues. I'm the man with the plan. If I don't take my shot, they'll all die. Period. End of discussion. Yet, in that way life flashes every moment of importance before your eyes before the fiber of your existence changes, I know the next few moments are going to make every decision I've ever made pale in comparison to the one I'm going to have to make in a little more than a minute.

Is it really possible I'm going to have to shoot through the body of my wife to take out the terrorist holding a room of people hostage on the night of our tenth wedding anniversary?

Resolution to punish those who dared to touch what is mine surges through me even as chatter picks up in my ear. With a grim determination, I tune out the static in my ear as I set my watch to count down from sixty.

Above the DC offices of Hudson Investigations, where I'm nestled into the roof to aim into the offices of McCallister Construction, motors from Blackhawk choppers are overhead spotlighting the target for us. The building, one of my wife's designs, comes alive under the spotlights. It lives and breathes along with the rest of us—holding steady even amid our panic as each pass increases my heart's fear. I force my mind to tune out the familiar scream of their blades—

a remembered sound from the hundreds of missions I successfully completed in the past.

The Blackhawks are there as backup to swoop in and perform a rescue or blow the enemy to bits, depending on what signal is given. Christ, I hope it isn't the second because if that's the case, I might just run into the building right before they do because there's nothing to live for if she's gone.

This isn't the frequent missions I was thrown into in Iraq or Afghanistan where my role was to protect the guys' six amid the familiar staccato of AK-47s being shot like they were firecrackers on the Fourth of July. Nor is it the controlled fury of the *Sea Force*, where desperation and broken souls of the human intelligence contractors threatened the safety of my team.

I'm not asking an old friend to rescue the infrastructure of our national security from a computer hack of catastrophic proportions. I almost wish it were a case of mistaken identity—another situation I could resolve with one hand behind my back after one of my agents went to ground after her identical twin was murdered.

No, this is a hell of my own making because of who and what I am —the path I chose to take in becoming director of the Agency. Because I am, the bastard frantically waving a gun around the room while my wife's wrapped up in enough explosives to take out the entire building thinks they have the goddamn right to fuck with what's mine.

Not for long.

My watch starts beeping, giving me a countdown.

Ten. Steady the bipod.

Nine. Lock in the magazine.

Eight. Slide my finger into place on the trigger.

Seven. Feel the callous where it nestles like an old friend.

Six. Inhale. Listen to the chatter silence.

Five. "Thorn, are you going to be able to take the shot?" is hissed through the comms link.

Four. Exhale. Come to a realization.

Three. I'm not afraid of dying. Even if I have to do it seconds after my wife.

Two. I mutter, "I've got it."

One. My finger squeezes.

The familiar recoil from my rifle kicks back into my shoulder. I don't have long to wait to find out if my life is over.

I'm just grateful as fuck I kissed her before I left the house this morning since I don't know if either of us will see tomorrow.

32

Present QUESTIONS

PARKER

"You're still with us," Fox notes.

"I'd rather be somewhere else."

"That's understood, sir. But on behalf of the Department of Justice, we appreciate your time today. We also appreciate this is a unique circumstance as this is not for hiring purposes, witness security, nor for you to join one of our Sensitive Investigative Units."

I wiggle my hands. "Then are we done? I have somewhere to be."

Deere and Pamola make their way over and begin to loosen the wires from the extremities to which they are attached. As they do, the camera recording our session shuts down, and the door unlocks. A friendly face steps inside even as I rub my wrists. *My second polygraph in as many days,* I think, wryly.

Fox takes note of the look on my face, and her own turns wary. "What's that look for?"

"Do I get a frequent flyer card to punch?" Turning to Cal, who is standing just inside the door, I wonder, "Think I can get out of my bi-annual poly for enduring this torture early?"

He snorts. "No. Besides your clearance is held through a different agency."

"Killjoy." He rolls his eyes at me before I ask the trio I've been working with all day, "I'd ask if it would be accepted in court, except that doesn't really matter, does it?"

Fox's smile turns malevolent. "No, sir, it doesn't. Whether or not your polygraph would hold up as testimony doesn't matter since they're all dead. The president just wanted to have it on record if there was any blowback."

"Understood." I push myself out of the chair and ask Cal, "Any changes?"

"Libby and Iris brought food a while ago. They said you should bring flowers."

I can't prevent the smile from spreading across my face. "Mind if we stop at the house?"

"Nope. Besides, tracksuits are not your best look."

Throwing him the finger, I'm about to storm past a gawking Fox, Pamola, and Deere. Instead, I pause and offer, "Let me know if you three are looking for a job. As of yesterday, I lost a team of polygraph examiners." Permanently. As in, they're in a federal prison somewhere I can't get to them—more's the pity. "You three did a hell of a job today."

Cal breaks in, "Despite who you were interviewing."

I roll my eyes. "How about you shut up and take me to my wife?"

He snaps off a salute. "Sir. Yes, sir." Then he mutters, "Only because *my* wife is with her."

Still, the minute we clear the door, Cal's hand comes down on the back of my neck and squeezes hard. We'll always be at each other's throats, but when it counts, when the waters are troubled, there are a few people Bethany and I know we can count on without question.

Who knew love would save all of us after the way we were all brought together, which was the travesty of it being torn apart?

33

In the PAST

Bethany

I sent Libby and Iris home. I want it to be just me and Parker when he finally makes it out of the interrogation into his actions last night. I knew he was completely justified in organizing the flurry of bullets that penetrated the windows of McCallister Construction.

After all, I was still breathing.

The scent of antiseptic fills my nose as I blink up at the ceiling. Because of our baby, I've been denying pain medication all day. Subsequently, my shoulder aches, a deep, throbbing pain radiating from the wound that knocked me out of the chair, permitting Parker to take a second shot—the kill shot that saved my life. I try taking a deep breath as I was instructed by the nurses earlier, but the shooting agony that caused my shoulder made me stop that torture.

Instead, I focus on even breaths that time along with the steady beeping of the one heart monitor I give a damn about—the baby's. The rhythm of Parker and my child's fragile life still fighting inside me, even after everything.

The memory hits me hard, sending a shiver down my spine. Parker's eyes. I can still see them—so full of pain and desperation, as he loomed over me in the ambulance, rifle tossed over his shoulder. He'd had no choice. I know that. I know he was doing what he had to do to save me, us, but that won't stop the memory from searing into his mind.

I wince as pain radiates through my shoulder. He shot me through the right arm to free me, the force knocking me from the chair. His bullet ripped through my shoulder and tore into the nuts of the man using me as a shield. If Parker hadn't taken that shot, I might not be here. Neither would our baby.

The door creaks open softly, and there he is. Parker. His face is etched with a mixture of exhaustion and exhilaration. I lift my left hand and beckon for him. Something shifts in the silvery depths of his eyes—relief, guilt?

Neither matters because clearly written on his face is the love I've been blessed with since he reentered my life over a decade ago.

"B." Just my nickname, but even on that, his voice breaks as he strides forward toward the bed. His eyes immediately veer to the heart monitor, where the steady beat of our baby's heart echoes in the small room. He lets out a shaky breath, and despite his strength to carry the world on his shoulders, I know him. I know he's about to break.

My lips, probably the only part of me that won't cause my shoulder to hurt, curve up in a smile. "Hey."

He sits beside me, hand trembling as he reaches for mine with the one bearing my ring. The other is clutching a bag with plastic containers sticking out of it. I want to grin because my Parker brought me flowers, but I'll wait. He needs to get whatever it is off his chest. I can feel the tension beneath his fingers, the barely contained storm of emotions he's trying so hard to hold back for me.

Finally, the storm breaks and when it does, it's like a crack of thunder outside. "I'm so sorry," he chokes out, voice cracking. "I'm so, so sorry, Bethany."

"You saved me," I whisper. "You saved us."

"It was because of me that you were in danger in the first place."

"You had no choice. You had to take the shot."

"I should've found another way," he mutters, his jaw tight. His hand squeezes mine. "You should never be in danger because of me."

"I'm here," I remind him, blinking back the tears that threaten to fall. "And our baby is still alive. Because of you."

His gaze drops to my belly, and the tension in his shoulders eases as he's lulled by the same sound I am—the beeping of the monitor. He didn't even know about the baby before everything went to hell. Now here we are—no longer just the two of us, but three. No longer a couple but a family.

His eyes soften and for the first time since walking into the room, I see the faintest hint of a smile. It is small, but it is there. That is enough for me to know we are going to be okay. *The last twenty-four hours are not how anyone should spend a decade together*, I muse as I pull my hand free from Parker's so I can run it through his dark hair. He leans into my touch.

"I love you," he whispers, his voice thick with emotion. "Both of you."

"I love you too. And we're going to be okay. All of us."

We are going to be okay. Maybe not today, maybe not tomorrow. But eventually, we would be okay. No matter what, we'll face it together. But... "Did you bring me flowers?" I demand.

For just a moment, we're transported to the date we first made love and how he frantically explained his mistake. What's between us is no mistake. It never has been, it never will be. Neither is the bouquet of chocolate roses that Parker presents me with while lying in my hospital bed. "Happy anniversary, B. I want at least a hundred more years with you."

I tug on his hair so he knows to come to me. Bracing himself on the hospital rails, he leans down far enough to kiss my lips. In that kiss, I feel the hard punch of desire, the strength of his protection, and the devotion of love.

I can't wait for our child to know what it feels like as well.

Epilogue

Bethany

"Mama!" shrieks our little girl, Cammie, as she toddles through our chilly backyard in McLean, Virginia. Named after both of our mothers, Camille Lorraine Thornton is the light of our lives. She's inherited my blond hair, but her eyes are entirely her father's.

So is her attitude, not to mention her propensity for getting into trouble.

But after twelve years of marriage, I'm an old pro of being able to handle the emotional roller coaster that comes with loving and being loved by a Thornton. I bend down and scoop her up. "What are you up to, sweetie?"

She beams a gap-toothed grin at me before waving a rose at me. She must have got it from her father because it's a perfect bloom with no thorns marring the stem. "Fors oos!" Her little face lights up as if she's just handed me a buried treasure.

I brush a lock of hair from her forehead and kiss her cheek, breathing in the sweet smell of sunshine and grass. "Thank you, my love. It's beautiful."

She wriggles in my arms, eager to return to what she was doing before being sent on this errand. The minute I set her down, she races in the direction of the house where my father is waiting to spoil her. In spite of the fact I know Parker and I created her, I still can't help but be in awe of the energy of this tiny human. "I swear she has more energy than six of us."

"You wouldn't be wrong about that, B. Then again, it might be my son draining all of yours." My husband's deep voice comes from the side. I can't prevent the smile that leaps to my face as I turn to face him.

It's been two years. Two years since the day Parker had been forced to pull the trigger and save us in the only way he could. Through my winter coat, I rub the spot where the scar on my shoulder lies out of habit, more than lingering pain. Yes, it's a physical reminder for both of us, but it's a wound that's healed over time. Through working with Dr. Rhumed, so did our lives. Parker had to get over his guilt, and I had to let go of my fear. Together, we learned coping mechanisms to discuss what happened with each other and ways to communicate that wouldn't put his job in jeopardy.

We're stronger because we struggled. Because of one day, one moment, our lives could have fallen apart. Instead, we didn't drown in the troubled water we found ourselves in. With help—professional, family, and friends alike—we made it safely to shore.

And now, we were here. Together. A family—an expanding one at that.

I turn, my lips already curving upward. He's still as handsome as the day I met him on the balcony in Mexico—maybe even more so.

He's always been ruggedly good-looking but with the hint of silver at his temples?

I shiver thinking, *Mine.* "Happy anniversary."

His arm wraps around my waist and his lips meet mine softly. "Happy anniversary."

I flick the rose back and forth. "Real ones?"

His eyes twinkle. "I didn't want Cammie begging for the sugar. I hid your real ones in our room."

My head falls back as I laugh loudly. "Good. I don't want to break tradition and not get my chocolate roses."

"No, it just means they'll be there for you when you get the munchies after I make love to you tonight."

"Hmm. That sounds even more delicious than the chocolate."

He tugs me tight against his body despite his wool overcoat and my maternity down jacket. His voice is laden with promise. "It sure does."

He kisses me then, slow and tender like he was savoring the moment. Savoring us. When we pull apart, his eyes are soft, filled with that same intensity that has been there ever since that long ago kiss in Playa del Carmen. But instead of the blankness after our first kiss, there's a shimmer in his due to a million different love-filled memories between us. Still, he's studying me closely, "What is it?"

"I love you."

"I love you too."

"We've come a long way, haven't we, B?"

"You mean from sharing booze over a balcony at a Brendan Blake concert?" My voice is laden with amusement, "We sure have."

Parker chuckles at being reminded of our auspicious beginnings. His expression turns serious for a moment. "You know, I never thought this would be my life. I never thought I'd get to have this."

I reach up to cup his face, running my thumb along the stubble on his jaw. "Neither did I," I admit. "Not after Mama died. But I'm so glad we were both wrong."

We stand together, wrapped in the quiet serenity of the chilly

February afternoon, the sun setting behind the trees and casting everything in a golden glow. I know in the world Parker and I inhabit, it's rare to find a moment's peace, but in moments like this there's one thing I know for certain.

It's right.

Our love is what makes it whole.

He nudges my chin back and brushes my lips with his. "How about a date once we put Cammie down?"

"What are you thinking?"

"How about a rematch at Spare Tavern?"

"Bowling? You want to go bowling? For our anniversary?" I clarify.

He scoops me up in his arms and begins making his way into the house. "I'm trying to be romantic—recreating our first date and all."

That's when I whisper in his ear, "How about we engage the soundproofing in our room and recreate the first time we made love instead?"

To which he replies, "I love your idea so much more."

"I just love you, Parker."

That's when he modifies a section of his wedding vows, vowing again to me. "I'll continue to crawl through deserts, fly through the skies, and swim through any troubled waters. All I want for the rest of my life is to be able to call you my wife. I love you too."

WANT MORE?

Want to dive beneath the waves and meet Parker and Bethany from different points of view?

Ripple Effect—Libby and Cal's Story
Flood Tide —Iris and Sam's Story

RIPPLE EFFECT

Calhoun "Cal" Sullivan has lived multiple lives by the time he's
assigned to teach an international political science class. It's a deception to recruit new team members devoted enough to sacrifice their
personal lives for righting the world's wrongs.

Cal catches sight of Libby on the quad. The cousin of his only friend,
Cal can't get involved because he's leaving.
She's worth everything, but maybe he isn't?

Elizabeth "Libby" Akin comes from old family money, though determined to build an independent life. One night, the walls surrounding
Cal slip. He asks her out only to break the date the next day.

But the way he says her name causes her skin to ripple with pleasure.

Cal renters her life, disturbed by the chilly woman and sharp words
that fall from her perfect lips. Her confidence causes him to seek her
out to see what lies between them.

He never realized falling in love with Libby would place him in such an untenable work situation. As profound as marrying her is, the secrets associated with an oath he's sworn to uphold begins to destroy the very person he loves most—Libby.

Long-term effects of miscommunication and sins of omission will change lives. Their marriage is hanging by a thread. Cal is forced to defend the choices he's made.

As for Libby, the lies she's been fed can't be washed away by a drink of water.

Not now.

One Click Ripple Effect today!

CHAPTER 1

Present DAY

Elizabeth

I've tried to leave this part of my life behind so many times. Over and over, I'm dragged back to rehash the memories of the worst days I've ever endured. *How many times can I do it before I say no more?* I think wearily. I'm proud to say I've moved on. It took years for me to get to where I am right now.

My husband, recognizing the tension whipping through my body, offers with complete seriousness, "We can leave."

I snicker. "'Cause that will go over well." I rub my hands up and down my arms, trying to warm myself.

He turns me to face him, and my slight baby bump brushes

against his muscular abs. "Like I give a damn about that. Especially now." His hand drops to caress my stomach tenderly.

I reach up and cup his cheek. Smoothing my hand back and forth over the bristles that tickle the inside of my palm, I murmur, "You need to shave."

"I ran out of time. This gorgeous pregnant woman had her way with me this morning. I was a wreck when she was done." His smile, the very first thing I noticed about him, makes my stomach flutter. Then again, maybe that's our baby kicking. Either way, I'm flooded with gratitude.

Now.

"I didn't notice you complaining," I tease.

He gives me a look rife with disbelief. "I may be called many things, but I hope I've grown out of my idiot stage."

Brushing my lips against his, I whisper, "I occasionally have to check. It took you a little longer than the average male."

Just as my husband's about to retaliate with some smart-ass comment, a door opens behind us. "Mrs. Sullivan? Dr. Powell is ready for you."

Cal doesn't let me go right away. "I'm right here, Libby. I've got you."

"I know." And I do; he's more than shown me that.

Concern flashes over his face. He opens his mouth but closes it just as quickly.

"What is it?" I ask. I don't have a lot of time before I need to be on the other side of that door.

Crushing me to him, he whispers directly in my ear, "You had a nightmare last night."

Surprised, I lean back in his strong arms. "I did?"

He nods solemnly. "And I know today's going to make things worse." The tick in his jaw betrays his calm demeanor.

Knowing I'm putting the schedule at risk, I wrap my arms around him and hold him as hard as I can. Cal buries his head in my neck.

"Even if they try to get to me in dreams, there's nothing for you to be afraid of."

"Why's that?" His voice is raw with remembered pain.

I search his tired eyes, which I can now see reflect his lack of sleep. Probably because he was standing guard over his family. Kissing him briefly, I pull out of his warm embrace and make my way to the door. I pause there and look back. "Because just like the first time I woke from my nightmare, you were there for me."

"I always will be. No matter what."

Without another word, I follow the young intern down the hall. Another person greets us before saying, "I'll take Mrs. Sullivan from here. How are you today?"

I smile and nod, but inside I'm screeching in maniacal laughter. Is anyone ever ready to have their emotions dissected like they're a frog in science class?

It takes another few minutes before I'm settled facing Dr. Powell. "It's a pleasure to see you again, Mrs. Sullivan."

"Libby, please," I correct him. I can't do this if we're going to stand on formality.

"Libby," he returns. "We left off yesterday talking about your background; you're an interior designer in the Washington, DC, area, correct?"

Smoothing a hand over my stomach, I nod. "Yes. A little less than four years ago now, my husband's company was bought out. We decided to relocate with the new owners."

"How does it feel to be back in Charleston?"

My eyes drift out the window overlooking the harbor. Sunlight glistens off the water. I shudder.

"Is strange an acceptable answer?"

"It is."

"Then let's go with that." The laugh I receive is appreciated, so I begin to relax.

Maybe it's too soon to do that.

"Libby, I can't help but notice you're expecting. "

"It's getting harder and harder for me to miss too," I joke, earning another chuckle.

"Is your family excited?"

"Beyond belief." I smooth a hand over my stomach, pulling my dress tighter.

"After everything you've been through, it must feel like a miracle," Dr. Powell says gently.

"Yes." I don't elaborate more because I suspect he will.

And I'm right.

"We're here for a reason, today, Libby. And this miracle is a perfect conclusion to it. I hate to take you back…"

"You don't have to," I tease. "We can just talk about how I plan on decorating the nursery."

He smiles. There's an edge of determination covered by a layer of sympathy to it that I abhor—not that I'd let him see. I don't need the sympathy; the families of the people who didn't survive do.

What I need is peace.

"I'd like to go back, Libby."

I shake my head, still wearing a smile. "What's the good in that?" For me, for Cal, for any of us?

"Context." Dr. Powell's words come back at me so succinctly, I want to roll my eyes, but I can hear Cal's voice in my head telling me to calm my sass.

Reaching for the unopened bottle of juice on the table next to me, I twist the cap off and take a small sip. Just a small one. I still can't consume liquids any faster than a tiny drink at a time. "How far back would you like to go?"

Flipping through the notes on his lap, he lifts off his glasses before asking, "What made you decide to take a trip on your own on the luxury cruise liner, *Sea Force*?"

Even knowing the question was coming, my heart sinks because I know of all the subsequent questions that are going to follow.

Cal was wrong. I was wrong. To keep raking this over the coals punishes more than just us.

Taking a deep breath, I admit, "Because I was certain my marriage was over."

After all, when a communication breakdown occurs in most marriages, there's always a ripple effect. But when it occurs on the international stage, and it involves a coordinated military rescue, well, the ripples are the size of a tsunami.

Plucking at my dress, a dress I chose to wear because it has sunflowers scattered on it, I remember the days leading up to when Cal gave them to me for the first time. It was right at the end of college, and every day seemed as beautiful outside as this one.

FLOOD TIDE

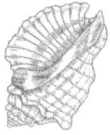

When linguistics expert Iris Cunningham met Samuel Akin, she fell irrevocably in love. She nursed a crush on her best friend's cousin. From an instant attraction, it grew to something much more during four long years at college.

She hid despair. He didn't feel the same.

Computer savant Samuel Akin denied his feelings for Iris until it was almost too late. Every time he was with her, a flood of emotion swept over him. He craved her yet feared he couldn't be with her.

She dragged his sense out of self to sea.

Their lives irrevocably entwine when love guides them first to an alliance, then marriage and family. They submerge themselves into a sworn existence few are privy.

Validating the half-truths demanded by the terms and conditions of their livelihood, threads of honor and integrity that bind them are tested. Yet while alternately maddened and delighted by the other, they take an opposing side over a fundamental disagreement.

They regret little about their lives together, but this?

When faced with accusations of betrayal, can they stand firm together against the waves crashing against them during the tides?

Or will their love be swept away in a wash of heartbreak?

ne Click Flood Tide today!

PROLOGUE

Present DAY

Iris

I'm emotionally exhausted.

In the last twelve months, I've spent so much time rising above accusations cast upon me for crimes I never committed when the ones I was forced to relive in mind were worse. Far worse.

I've learned the hard way when the people you have to cross are faceless, it matters far less than if you know their names, let alone if you're directly connected to their hearts and souls. And this makes the second time I've withstood this type of inquisition.

A piece of my long curl escapes the clip I twisted my mass of hair into before we left our home this morning but before I can reach up to shove it back, his fingers are there gently tucking the wayward curl behind my ear. Like he's done countless times.

Sam trails his fingers down my cheek before running them down my arm. Intuitively, our fingers tangle together as we wait to be called back. Silently, I study them as they interlock tightly at the webbing. Since the morning I woke up in a strange hospital, he's always held my hand like this, fiercely. As if he was afraid someone would try to rip my hand from his grasp before he had a chance to tether me to him.

I study his hands not without the same awe I always feel. Sam's hands have been able to bring me incomparable pleasure and yet, they've been used as a tool for undeniable destruction. I apply pressure so he feels the pinch of my wedding ring, a reminder of the vows we took together all those years ago.

And have held steadfast to.

It was a near-constant pain that lanced through me as I endured allegations of breaking apart our family using more than my mind, more than my voice, my heart. I shake my head, even now fervently denying the charges. Not true in any manner, but to right the wrongs inadvertently committed to the people I love before God any country, I agreed to take this step.

My husband did as well.

Because before our own comfort, someone else's needs comes first. And it's long overdue she has this peace of mind to put some closure on this part of her—our—past.

His lips brush against the back of my fingers when he lifts my hand to his lips. "It's graduation day."

"You hope," I retort. But I can't prevent the curve of my lips because I know he's right.

"I can't believe we made it this far without you cursing more."

"Sam," I warn him, but I can't contradict him. Reliving over twenty years of our past—when we could share it—has been incredibly emotional.

"Especially in Russian and French. You seem to enjoy the punch in those words," he teases.

I sniff, but don't bother with a verbal retort. After all, how am I supposed to argue when this man knows me like no other person? We fell in love, created a family, and have faced death together. And that's only what's happened so far. Knowing we cast our future in a world that's murky at best, we relish every moment on our island of solace with each other. And along the way hurt caused against our loved ones has caused our own marital struggles.

But like most others, we hung on past the rough seas into smooth sailing.

I lay my head on Sam's shoulder and bring him back to his original statement. "You hope it's our graduation day."

"I'm highly optimistic. Rachel asked me to help plan something," he murmurs, keeping his voice low in deference to the other people milling about the large waiting room.

I roll my eyes. "Just tell me it doesn't involve her cooking." One skill our daughter didn't inherit from her maternal great-grandmother was her ability to devastate the senses with food. *No, Rachel is absolutely mine and Sam's. ,* I admit silently. In fact, I'd do anything for family just short of murder. After all, if I was willing to give myself over to this torture, I'm willing to do anything to purge the demons that have plagued our family for far too long.

Ones everyone was certain we'd all moved past until...

Sam's always been able to calculate where my mind wanders to. "What she asked us to do just made us stronger, Iris."

Ignoring any eyes that may be trained on us—either the human or electronic kind— I tip my head back and press my lips to my husband's. Like the first time, the flash of heat leaps between us. Despite our rather auspicious surroundings, it makes me want to sink my fingers deep into his sable-colored hair to deepen this kiss. Hell, any kiss so long as it's Sam's lips touching mine.

And judging by the sparkle in his eyes as he pulls away, he knows it. "Later," he mouths.

I pout, pretending an insult I don't feel. Because like so many things in our marriage, he's right. Now isn't the time to lose ourselves in one another.

I twirl a lock of still dark waves around my finger as I contemplate what's going to be said in just a few moments. Sam might have been right, but so many times he was wrong, refusing to listen on important things.

Things that have come back to haunt us.

The door swings open. A young man wearing a buttoned vest steps out holding a thick teal folder. Every time I see it, I'm reminded me of the waters in the Cooper River when the sunlight hits it just so as it passes Sam's family home—Akin Hill. "Mr. and Mrs. Akin? Are you ready?"

We both stand, still holding onto one another's hands. Our future is just a few hours ahead. We've paid our penance, made our apologies. I can't deny when Sam's hand releases mine to drop to the small of my back to guide me through the door to greet the person on the other side, I'm bolstered by the support it provides me.

"IF I NARROW MY EYES, it would be so easy to imagine you the first time I saw you," Saw declares outrageously from where he's sprawled across the leather Chesterfield. His arm is draped casually across the back as if this isn't the most important meeting of our lives.

Which it is.

I remind him, "You ignored me for the better part of three years before you acknowledged my existence."

"I wouldn't say that."

"You're right." I agree immediately. His face morphs into a look of shock over my admission before I continue, "You treated me exactly like Libby. I had all of these overwhelming emotions for you and you kept petting me on the head. Proverbially of course."

He scowls. "I didn't treat you like Libby." Libby is Sam's first cousin and was my college roommate for four years. She was, and is today, my best friend. The two of us are closer than many of the biological relationships I've had a bird's eye to in the Akin family.

"Of course, that's the point you fixate on, Samuel." I roll my eyes skyward.

That's when he throws out, "Maybe you should have tried harder, Iris." His green eyes, eyes our daughter inherited, sparkle at me outrageously.

And I scream incoherently. In all of the trips we've made to this very office, I've never been so grateful for the soundproofing as I have at this one singular moment. After I finish with the primal shriek, I realize the pressure valve has loosened. Sam, grins at me. "Feel better?"

"Strangely, yes." I drop down onto the sofa. His arm immediately curls around me, like it had merely been waiting to curl me into his side.

"Your ancestors—both sides— used to let loose some of those war cries before they'd go into battle."

"Like I'm not aware of that?"

But suddenly I'm giggling.

"What's so funny?" He asks.

"You just reminded me of something I once said to Libby before we ever got together."

"What was it?"

I glance to the door behind the desk. Since it hasn't opened, I begin to tell him.

LOVED THE DEVOTION SERIES?

Addicted to Bodyguard/Military romance in a workplace setting
where a main character overcomes an emotional past?
Then dive right into the Amaryllis Series next.
Available in Amazon/KU!

AMARYLLIS SERIES
Free to Dream
Free to Run
Free to Rejoice
Free to Breathe
Free to Believe
Free to Live
Free to Dance
Free to Wish
Free to Protect
Free to Reunite

NEWSLETTER

Sign up for my newsletter to get an exclusive prequel to the Amaryllis Series as well as access to exclusive bonus scenes after new books release.

ACKNOWLEDGMENTS

Nathan, you're my touchstone—the one constant willing to rescue me from the ever surging wave. I love you.

To my son, you can get through anything thrown at you. I believe you and your big heart will prevail.

Mom, thank you for reminding me I'm strong and I was inspired by the strongest woman there is. I love you.

Jen, I'm so grateful you found your HEA. I love you forever. XOXO.

My Meows, there is one line in here JUST for you. I love all of you so much.

To my "daughter," for all the mutual cackling and stories we shared while I wrote this book. Love you and my Cakes.

Amy, Kristin, and Dawn, One word, romcom. This is as close as it gets. Love all of you so much.

Amy, you have made this life so much easier for me. Love you.

To Missy Borucki, your messages are the best. I laugh every time I get your messages. LOL. XOXO.

To Holly Malgieri, my twin. Hulken! Life is that good to us. Who would have ever thought I could humanize Thorn to be funny? LOL. Love you!

To photographer Wander Aguiar, Andrey Bahia, Jenny Flores, and Donna Lathan, thank you so much!

To my cover designer, Deborah Bradseth, absolute perfect. XOXO

To Gel, at Tempting Illustrations, you make everything shine!

To the team at Foreword PR, thank you. MUAH.

Linda Russell, every day we are together is a better day. Thank you for being so much a part of my life.

Finally, my thanks to all of you, I am overwhelmed by your emails, your comments, and reviews. Thank you for your support and for choosing to enjoy my words.

ABOUT THE AUTHOR

It began when Tracey made up stories in her head as she biked around her neighborhood in Connecticut. Writing, always a passion, interfered with her life when she started rewrote the ends of books instead of finishing college assignments. After all, what was more important, a happily ever after or Greek mythology?

Eventually, she realized the answer was both when she wrote the Amaryllis Series.

Tracey's collection of contemporary romance and women's fiction is available on Amazon.com and free on kindleunlimited. This includes her best-selling Amaryllis Series, Midas Series and Glacier Adventure Series. She has over twenty-five books in print and has participated in several anthologies for reader pleasure as well as charity.

Tracey is dedicated to her own happily ever after, having been married since 2007. She and her husband have one son who is as addicted to his Fortnite as his mama is to coffee.

When she's not busy with her family or writing, Tracey can be found in her home in north Florida plotting her next story, training for a runDisney event, and feeding her addiction to HGTV.

www.ingramcontent.com/pod-product-compliance
Lightning Source LLC
Chambersburg PA
CBHW060647260626

47161CB00008B/3032